THE
RULE
OF
STEPHENS

THE
RULE
OF
STEPHENS

TIMOTHY TAYLOR

DOUBLEDAY CANADA

Doubleday Canada and colophon are registered trademarks of Penguin Random House Canada Limited

LIBRARY AND ARCHIVES CANADA CATALOGUING IN PUBLICATION

Taylor, Timothy L., 1963-, author
    The rule of Stephens / Timothy Taylor.

Issued in print and electronic formats.
ISBN 978-0-385-68736-2 (softcover).--ISBN 978-0-385-68737-9 (EPUB)

    I. Title.

PS8589.A975R85 2018   C813'.6   C2017-904637-3
                                              C2017-904638-1

Cover and text design: Leah Springate
Cover images: (clouds) Robert Kneschke/EyeEm/Getty Images; (birds) SkillUp/ Shutterstock.com

Printed and bound in the USA

Published in Canada by Doubleday Canada,
a division of Penguin Random House Canada Limited

www.penguinrandomhouse.ca

10 9 8 7 6 5 4 3 2 1

Penguin
Random House
DOUBLEDAY CANADA

In memory:

Richard Taylor   (April 23, 1922 – April 8, 2016)
Jill McDougall   (Aug 15, 1936 – May 10, 2016)
Kent Enns   (Aug 5, 1964 – July 13, 2016)

—

And what the dead had no speech for, when living,
They can tell you, being dead: the communication
Of the dead is tongued with fire beyond the language
    of the living.

— T.S. ELIOT, LITTLE GIDDING

The Rule of Stephens *n.* an axiom holding that the observable universe works in one of two mutually exclusive ways: (1) strictly in accordance with materialist principles such as those advanced in the work of Stephen Hawking, or (2) by rules providing for the paranormal aberrations manifest in the work of Stephen King.

ONE

I said this can't be me
Must be my double

—LEONARD COHEN, *I Can't Forget*

THE SIGNIFICANCE OF BEING A SURVIVOR, in the case of Air France Flight 801, for a long time lay in the simple fact that there should have been no survivors. At least, for a long time, that's what Catherine Bach considered the crucial element of the story. The press felt differently. News accounts in the aftermath of the doomed Chicago-bound flight focused on the unexplained circumstances surrounding the crash, the possibility of lightning or some other external impact, the failure for six weeks to find the flight recorder until it was eventually fished out of Brittas Bay off the east coast of Ireland not at all far from where the big plane went down. One account of the incident hinged on the rumour that an extra, unauthorized pilot was in the cockpit of the Airbus A380-800 at the time. And that gave rise to a storm of follow-up press and blog speculation all addressed to the mysterious and tantalizing possibility of a fifth man. *#AF801TheFifthMan.*

The public meanwhile—and Catherine knew this term to be a polite cover over the more accurate description *complete strangers*— seemed interested only in the perceived life-dividend of survival. As the months stretched to a year, and then on out towards two full years afterwards, Catherine became wearily familiar with a common line of questioning, maybe linked to the fact that the accident had happened just before New Year's. Didn't she feel very blessed? Was she not now filled with purpose and meaning? Did life not shimmer with possibility in the wake of those moments when possibility itself was so very nearly snuffed out entirely?

Catherine, who generally did not mind disappointing people, nevertheless struggled to be as direct as she might have liked in response to these questions. She'd be stopped on the street. She'd find a hand on her arm in the lineup to pay at the grocery store. Cab drivers caught her in the rear-view mirror, did a double take before launching in. And she'd find herself smiling weakly, wondering if she was perhaps projecting some insufficiency of gratitude.

But as important as all that speculation might have been to those people and to those newspapers and magazines, their voracious curiosity missed the feature of the crash that would never be explained by data or the evidence of any one survivor's life. And that was the fact (and Catherine considered it a fact) that the six survivors of AF801 were supposed to be dead. Statistically speaking, staying with science. The way that plane went down—shredding the clouds, salting the shore, boiling the sea—there was just no case to be made that anyone in that thin-skinned aluminum coffin should still be alive.

Of course, things do happen implausibly on occasion. Catherine had studied family medicine and toxicology, then worked at a walk-in clinic on Vancouver's Downtown Eastside for eight years before leaving practice at age thirty-four to start her own business. Catherine knew about probabilities and bell curves and the occasions on which the very limits of the likely were reached and exceeded. She'd seen a woman shipped off to emerg and then surgery for the removal of what turned out to be 343 gallstones. She'd treated a two-year-old who had fallen three storeys into the improbable safety of an open dumpster full of shredded legal documents. She'd lost count of the supra-combinatory overdoses—people amped and kitty-flipping, bananoed and shabued, so past grey zones they were falling through the twilight sub-mantles of death itself—who had yet been brought back to life. If street medicine taught you anything, it was that the human animal did survive on occasions when rational analysis told you it shouldn't.

Catherine understood that much. But as those calendar leaves peeled away and fluttered out of frame, she also could not shake the feeling that probability could not entirely account for her situation. And she wondered if she felt that all the more intensely, more than the other five survivors, because only Catherine had walked away. She wasn't unscratched. But she fell from the clouds to earth and was only scratched.

Catherine didn't like to talk about the details of the crash. Even in therapy, which she'd tried briefly just after the first anniversary, Catherine had spoken carefully, circumspect, omitting parts. Even as difficulties had been mounting and all tides in life seemed to be ebbing hard against her, when she was taking Paxipam to sleep every night, she did sit and squirm in the deep leather chair of the therapist's office and speak carefully around the topic of what she'd seen, what she remembered, but never recounting the details of what she still dreamed nightly. Scenes as if through a strobe light. The massive noise of the explosion and the roiling of black smoke in the cabin. The drink trolley that smashed out of nowhere and into her legs before there was even a sensation of falling. A sudden awareness of herself pinned to the ceiling of the cabin. Sounds and smells and pains bleeding into one another. And at the very moment of tipping, at the top of that long and earnest fall, some stiffness, some *realness* seemed to leach out of the structure around her. The plastic tray tables and leather seats, the aisle carpeting and all the members of aluminum and steel that made up the plane's most essential inner workings, all these seemed to lose form and rigidity, liquefying long before contact with the hard ocean below. As they began to fall, she broke through layers of sensation, cutting the night sky over Ireland, disintegrating as they went, wings detaching as if the plane were moulting, the tail section floating away and the cabin awash with debris and bodies. She was pasted to the ceiling, pinned there above her ticketed seat, and she felt only a terrible separation. It would have been impossible to explain if Catherine had ever tried to discuss it. A separation from herself, like being able to feel herself twice, at once here and gone, one actual and one potential Catherine Bach. One present, one future conditional. The G-forces seeming to push right through her, gravity working its last wish to both split and unify. *To black-hole me*, that's what she thought. *To pull me out of myself and deposit me in two places on opposite sides of the universe at once.* And in the moment that thought struck her, she hallucinated vividly, the air around her seeming to fill instantly with black shapes, thudding and beating their wings. Birds, an instant shroud of them, black wings and beaks and claws that touched the skin of her arms and legs and face, their shuddering bodies close and cold. And Catherine fell in this shroud of black birds towards the sea, understanding the creatures to have burst into existence directly from her chest, spiralling out and away from her, but having emerged directly from her own heart.

A miracle. That was the other thing that people said, cycling back to the idea of her great blessing, the beneficence of heaven. And here the published photographs did not help her, as they tended to support the miracle reading. Even Catherine looked at those images, the most iconic of which were taken on an iPhoneX by a twelve-year-old girl from Indianapolis on holiday in Wicklow County, and realized that otherwise reasonable people would indeed reach for something beyond the natural world to explain how she'd stood up and walked away from that littered, pebbly shoreline, with the heaving mound of the cockpit and a length of double-tiered fuselage still bobbing in the bay behind her.

You walked away! Every day you must wake up so grateful! The implication and attendant obligation were clear—Catherine would need to do something very special with the tanked-up gift card that the Fates had apparently hand-delivered to her. *You must have incredible plans.* Well, she did. But she'd had plans before too.

The other survivors, significantly, Catherine thought, had each been badly injured, each hospitalized, taking weeks and months to re-enter the world as best they could. She thought of them often, more than work really allowed her the time for, and then more and more, in part because difficulties at work seemed to demand it. She'd avoided knowing the names, but had a single secret artifact from the ill-fated flight, a seat map, six seats marked with yellow highlighter.

12B, 18E, 20F, 63B, 70F.

Her own seat was 2L. But it seemed to her those five others, by being injured, by struggling for survival, those five had also obeyed the bell curve a degree more than she had. They'd paid a crucial courtesy to luck, however unconscious the genuflection, a courtesy she had herself not paid. And it was for that failure on her part that luck seemed recently to have turned against her.

Catherine didn't like thinking this way. Luck, fate, destiny. These were conceits, offensive to rational thought and logic. The universe, like the human body, was complex and on occasion surprising. But it remained an ordered and structured thing. The Rule of Stephens, she'd lectured her sister, Valerie, as far back as when they were still in high school. That would be Stephen Hawking or Stephen King. There were the laws of physics and then there was everything else. You had to choose which set of rules explained life best.

Valerie, three years younger and an aspiring stage actress in her teen years, had always seemed faintly dissatisfied with natural explanations. She was then, in Catherine's memory, always yearning mystery, even tragedy into the world. *Such a redhead*, people would say about Valerie, but never about Catherine, who shared the same strawberry ginger hair inherited from their mother, the same fine, fair features and intense green eyes. Catherine remembered the lunches she and her sister had shared in an empty chem lab, half an hour over salads they made together before school. Half an hour before Valerie's friends came to find her and Catherine herself turned to whatever homework needed her attention, whatever book was on the go. She recalled one occasion, running late, a mid-term afternoon in April or May. She'd rushed in flustered and talking already about the injustice of her English teacher's marking scheme: *so subjective, so lacking in rigour*. And there was Valerie wiping away tears, trying to cover up the horoscope that she'd been reading.

Friends can be deceiving. And as Saturn squares with Venus, beware the one friend who . . .

Valerie distraught. Catherine instantly furious. Saturn said no more about Valerie's chances in love or friendship than it did about Catherine's English grades. There was this matter of physical causality, Catherine ranted. And since she was also carrying around a copy of *A Brief History of Time* that year, in the cause of sisterly, protective love she resorted to it. That really was her up at the chalkboard drawing cones that met at their points, trying to explain how the speed of light quite tightly proscribed what could affect a given moment, just as it limited how a given moment could affect the future. Catherine with chalk in her hand, drawing pictures, trying to explain Hawking's "hypersurface of the present" just as the lab door burst open and Valerie's drama club friends poured in.

The one in the lead was lean with broad shoulders and a narrow waist, brown T-shirt, golden, close-cut hair. He had dark brown eyes and an expression of endless amusement. He'd played Paul in the school's musical production of *Misery* that year. Catherine had seen it and could not dispute that the young man could lie in a bed, fake broken ankles and still sing like a lark.

He looked at Catherine, the older, weirder sister. Catherine felt that exact assessment in the gaze. The one who freckled more. The one with glasses, always toting books. To this young man, they must have looked like opposites in that moment.

He looked at the chalkboard, laughing a musical laugh.

"Time cones?" he said.

Then he took Valerie by the hand and pulled her towards the door.

"Stephen Hawking or Stephen King," Catherine called after them, her face red but refusing to feel ashamed of what was right. "The world runs by the rules of one of them. And you have to choose, people!" And nothing in the universe was going to rise against that statement. No fact then known or to be proven in future, woven as all such facts must be in the warp and woof of the universe's magnificent and rational unfolding. She had been so sure.

Where had that dead certainty gone? At work, invariably, in a slow but undeniable way, Catherine would sense herself in branching moments with nothing like her typical clarity of plan and vision, ranked options with outcome probabilities assigned. And her eyes would drift to one of the warehouse windows, and in the long light of the late afternoon, in the blue shadows of shining buildings, on the flanks of the black and looming north shore hills, she saw something pixelated there, some early-blooming seed crystal of doubt.

And not from lack of data, either. Data Catherine had in spades, in heaving seas. That failing sense of certainty came instead from another, distinctly more troubling source. She shared this with no one, not even Valerie. But from quite early after it happened, she began to have the strange sense of something newly alive in the world, something with opposing polarity. An opposite, she thought, a phantom with no phase or physics. A force, it seemed, at work on the project of balancing luck's ledger, betting against her. Running up the odds in some unfavourable way, and threatening to win too, it had to be said. On a couple of recent occasions, threatening to win big.

Didn't she feel very blessed? Was she not now filled with purpose and meaning? Did life not shimmer with possibility in the wake of those moments when possibility itself was so very nearly snuffed out entirely?

They asked their question with wide eyes and open hearts. A good number of them wanted to hug her. They'd read the whole story. They knew the gory truth, the body count. They'd been online and read the black box transcript, heard the recording of the pilot's strange last words. *We are coming apart. We are . . .* and then this, in what was described as a scream from the centre of a cloud of squelch, at exactly 10:30 p.m.: *We're splitting. We're splitting.*

No bang to speak of at impact. No sound at all at the dreaded *moment of.* Only impact, radical and entire. Those black birds swarmed around her. The black hole opened, and out came fire and water and death to all but those lucky six.

12B, 18E, 20F, 63B, 70F . . .

And all the way up front to her own suite in first class, 2L—which struck her now as an embarrassment, that just before disaster she'd thought to accept this favour from an over-ingratiating booking agent, an upgrade from economy to radical indulgence. *We're empty up there. You'll like it. Trust me.* That was her accepting the unpaid upgrade, now living with the knowledge that whoever had taken her seat in economy had died in her stead.

Did the other five do the same? Did they have worn seat plans over which they pored in the dead of night? Did they silently reach for answers, wondering at the impossible reasoning of it all? In hotel lobbies. In boardrooms. Driving the freeway. Waiting to board a train. Did they all travel by train now? Had they sworn off flying, delaying meetings, putting everyone out of sorts, driving three hours to Seattle when a meeting with potential investors could not possibly be Skyped or avoided?

Two years later, two years into the downward spiral of what was supposed to be her recovery, her rebirth, Catherine Bach learned that at least one of them did. Sitting on her couch, stroking her old tabby cat Toby. And she thought: things happen for reasons. Effects are caused. And here comes a cause that she could have perhaps squinted her eyes and seen coming earlier, approaching her steadily all that time. A speck, then a shape, then a human form coming in across the waves, the beach and the dunes, through the sifting fronds of Irish beach grass. Only then a sound. Pinprick in the ear, a cascade of synthetic bells.

And now her phone ringing. Her personal cell. A number only a few people close to her knew and it wasn't any of them calling.

It was 70F.

DIYagnosis

CATHERINE BACH WAS THIRTY-FIVE YEARS OLD when AF801 went down. In the year prior, she had managed to take a single week off, a poorly considered trip to Cabo San Lucas with a man she'd only been out with a couple of times. Liam. They shared a room, had sex once but went to sleep in separate beds. He hated the food. They broke up on the plane home, amicably enough, and she hadn't heard from him since. Other than that, life was work. It had been a single frantic year since Catherine had stopped her practice at the clinic to plow all her still-meagre savings into DIYagnosis Personal Health Systems, a next-generation health-tracking wearable that monitored user vital signs and that would—assuming they succeeded in building and testing the various prototypes—feed back to the user a whole range of vital stats, from blood pressure to respiration rates, BMI, T-cell counts, liver enzymes.

Know your body. Change your world.

But even those weren't the features that had insiders excited. (And they were excited. The DIY Warehouse out on Terminal Avenue behind the train station was buzzing and bouncing late into every evening: thirty-eight employees, three interns. They were all there weekends, hived off in team meetings at the whiteboard pods, playing ping-pong, huddled in twos and threes in the soundproof teepee that sat in the centre of the space.) What really had those on the inside excited were the features in development— skunkworks stuff, deep secret, need to know—that stood to completely reinvent the relationship people had with this business of their own health.

A health diagnostic wearable on steroids so you'll never have to be.

Specifically: diagnostic modules in development that promised to read tumour markers, detect pre-cancerous tissue, early-alert risk factors for a range of disorders including diabetes, seasonal flu, malaria, meningitis, Crohn's, hepatitis A through C, cirrhosis, encephalitis and most recently Alzheimer's. There were molecular signatures for many of these. Ghostly geometric anomalies, mitochondrion tics and tells. And around the world physicists and molecular biologists were just now cracking these codes. Catherine's big idea had been to bundle that knowledge, load it up directly into the body, then give the user a dashboard on which their own physiology might be monitored, read in graphics, animations and text.

Your body talks. We'll help you listen.

"One subcutaneous chip and half these cases go away." This was a long-time colleague back when Catherine was still working at the clinic on the Downtown Eastside. He was standing next to her behind the counter, looking out across a crowded reception area full of downcast faces, rounded shoulders—a roomful of slumped resignation, noting that the master-deficit in front of them was early information.

Catherine had just sent a patient away with abdominal pains and a referral to a GI specialist. Call it eight weeks and a cost of half a million dollars to the system by the time they were done. Prospects? Well, not great. By that point the man's stomach was digesting itself, which was going to happen if you ate handfuls of ibuprofen morning and night—dialing down the pain from severe gout—such that you opened bleeders in your pylorus and duodenum. Catherine remembered it was a grey Vancouver day outside. There had been a freak October snowfall the night before that had melted off. The windows were steamed over. It was uncomfortably warm in the clinic but too cold outside to open the windows. Everything was humid and claustrophobically close, and Catherine saw something as clear as an actual vision in front of her: a warning light on a dashboard that that might have really helped had it lit up a few years prior.

"One chip," the colleague continued. Harvey was his name. "Some computer somewhere. Gout isn't exactly a stealth bomber. Uric acid. Urate crystals. Orange alert. Red alert. I mean, we're not talking mesothelioma here. Gout pretty much announces itself. Someone should really invent something. You maybe. Weren't you in engineering before med school?"

Of course, Harvey's words alone hadn't tipped the scale. There had been a sequence of steps and conversations that led to her changing first her mind and then her life. Her friend Phil, whom she'd known since university, hadn't exactly been against it, but registered his caution when it came up. A start-up, really? Hadn't medicine been her dream?

"Ever since your mother died," he said.

They were sitting at a bar, as they sometimes did Thursdays after work.

"Ever since my mother died?" Catherine said, wondering if he was right. Twelve years since cancer had taken her far too early at the age of fifty-nine. Her mother's death had been a deeper agony than Catherine could ever have imagined given the degree to which they had by that point drifted. Maybe that really had been the reason she went back to school. The motive for medicine. Saving lives. But if that was the case—and she had to acknowledge that Phil was generally right in these matters—then it motivated her now too. Knowing what the body already knows, building something that literally everybody on earth could use.

"I'm thinking big all of a sudden," Catherine said. "I mean, what's not to like about this idea?"

"Put it that way and I can't think of anything," Phil said, having listened to her speak with that wry and unflappable smile. *Consigliere*, she'd once called him. He'd nodded gravely, as if accepting a lifetime assignment. But the fact was he looked the part, handsome in a slightly lost way, with a round, boyish face and hair cut stubble-short to hide the male-pattern baldness. His father was Bahamian, mother English. He'd come to Vancouver to do his undergrad, then got into law school, got the articling position, got associate and then partner and never left. He said he liked Vancouver in part because people thought he was black.

"Or Libyan," he'd once told her, early in their friendship. "I get that too."

"Well we know you aren't Libyan," Catherine had said. "But wasn't your father black?"

Sure, yeah. Maybe. Phil explained that his father had insisted until the moment of his untimely demise in a deep-sea powerboat racing accident that he was, in fact, Scottish. "That's all he'd say," Phil said with a characteristic shrug. "Plus he talked pretty much exactly like Sean Connery, so who was going to argue?"

Phil was, in any case, perfect for his role. He advised people. He made them aware of the legal landscapes just beyond their range of vision. He was superb at unpacking people and their problems, finding solutions that would never have occurred to clients previously. And so, as *consigliere*, with Catherine he had a tendency to probe, to ask his questions. How was she doing?

Oh fine. Of course she was fine. Busy as hell but wasn't everybody? Catherine spoke with an airy nonchalance she was pretty sure Phil saw through. Of course she was nervous, but she was also excited. Phil didn't really display either of those psychological states very often. He was himself so seemingly secure and settled with his thriving practice, his big house in West Van, nearly empty since the divorce. But neither was he the sort to call her on it. That wasn't Phil. Her *consigliere* segued seamlessly then, away from how she was doing and on to something he'd just read online that

THE RULE OF STEPHENS   •   17

morning. He did this a lot. And she liked it. He curated the world for her. Articles from *The Guardian*, *The Times*, Buzzfeed Animals. Here was an interesting one. Something about how you could use the human body to make electrical power. Something about how you could turn a person's stomach into a microbattery. It showed up on Digg.

Down in Gastown over beers. Irish pub. Ranks of colourful tap handles. Dead Frog. Four Winds. Steel and Oak. Red Arrow. Red Collar. Red Truck. Conversation roaring around them. Hops and barley in the air. Catherine was staring at Phil. Staring really hard.

"Cate," he said. "What?"

"Battery how?" Catherine said to Phil. Her hand on his arm, nails just now biting into the silver-grey Paul Smith worsted.

How the pieces snapped together Catherine wasn't sure she'd ever understand. All she knew for sure was that she'd mentally written her letter of resignation to the clinic by the time Phil dropped her home. Kiss on the cheek. She was so preoccupied she didn't remember saying thanks, goodnight. However it had happened, it happened very fast. The answer to one of the questions that had been lingering since Harvey aired out his big idea about a recon drone launched into the body for the purposes of watching the shifting weather systems there.

The question was: what would the smart chip use for power?

"You swallow it."

This was Catherine a week later talking to Yohai, a friend from her years in engineering. Yohai the wannabe rabbi-kibbutznik with his flowing beard and yarmulke, T-shirts and combat pants. Steel-framed glasses with scratched lenses. Catherine was pretty sure Yohai had never been to a synagogue, much less Israel. More crucially for her purposes, this old friend was under-plying his engineering and coding trade on a system to automate user payment on public transit. The only part of the job Yohai really seemed to enjoy was attracting attention from cranks who thought his system would be used to track people.

"Sorry, swallow what?"

It could not have pleased Catherine more to have snuck up on Yohai with this idea.

The sensor, the monitor. You could get it down to a quarter the size of an aspirin. And attached to it, at about the size of a grain of sand, a component made of copper and magnesium. "Copper, magnesium. Plus stomach acid. There's your battery."

Yohai thinking hard. "How do you stop it flushing out of the system?"

Exactly the right question, though here you had some highly proprietary information. The mooring technology, Catherine called it, which of course all still had to be developed and tested. But there were patents available for purchase that it seemed to Catherine had never quite been combined in the right way before.

Yohai looked dubious. "Subcutaneous would be more stable. And you could power it with a mini-cell easy, like a pacemaker."

Sure, Catherine agreed. But then you had to cut people. Surgery would mean lower uptake. Here you had an almost invisible pill you could take with a glass of water.

Yohai staring. "Lifespan?"

Well, to be determined. But Catherine thought a year before the battery components failed and the device was naturally evacuated. Then you'd pop another pill and off you'd go.

She had him. His eyes were shining behind those glasses.

"So it gathers whatever data, then extracts." Yohai was seeing it. He was imagining the future. "Like a wristwatch or pendant, some kind of wearable. Or a skin patch."

Phone app, Catherine said. Device to phone. Phone uploads data to the cloud. Cloud automates reports and alerts back to users.

"Or maybe it downloads to the family doctor of record," Yohai said. "Or to our own staff panel of experts. Customized health advice. Nano-scaled hyper-personalized health management. Grab that domain."

He was already building the thing having heard about five minutes' worth of the idea. And Catherine sat back and watched with real pleasure as his brain jumped gears.

A couple of months. Three maybe. To Catherine this was a blurry period, time accelerating with her thought processes. She had her meagre savings. She secured a bank line of credit and assembled patents, acquired in as stealthy and hasty a fashion as Phil could accommodate. And, most importantly, she had her team. Yohai. Designer Hapok, who'd just exited his last start-up, a nootropics play involving memory enhancement. Kalmar, fresh off the plane from San Francisco (Reykjavik before that), in Vancouver by his own account to snowboard, to mountain bike, to do the Grouse Grind and make his package.

"You say *Reykjavik* like that's a qualification," Catherine said to Yohai, when he showed her Kalmar's CV. Who puts his picture on his CV? Like it was 1982. Brooding. Nice chin, admittedly. Something intense in the eyes. Twenty-nine years old. "And did he actually say *package*? He does realize nobody gets rich doing this kind of thing. He knows I'm in it for the *ideals*."

"That's not exactly motivating leadership," Yohai said. "Just saying."

More to the point, he noted, directing her attention down the page: database design, markets expert. Kalmar was a user-base and subscription ninja. He'd been at Hulu during the first phase of their explosive growth.

"Oooh," Catherine said. "Why leave?"

"Videos are videos," Yohai said. "A person's health is on another level."

—

Nootropics. Catherine wondered about that. Did those brain enhance-
ments ever really work? Wasn't gingko biloba basically a placebo?

Hapok laughed and shrugged his enormous shoulders when she
asked him. He made a certain impression, this one. He brought a
Vizsla named Cooper to work with him, who frequently sat in his
lap during meetings. He also appeared to lift weights, and a con-
siderable amount of them. With folded arms, his bald head and gold
earring, he looked quite a bit like Mr. Clean.

"Yes and no," Hapok said in response to the placebo question.
Which seemed like the only fair answer. All four of them in the room
together, finally. Her apartment on Ogden Avenue in Kitsilano. Her
living room with its long view of Kitsilano Beach through the glass.
A cobalt sea beyond, flecked with its countless licks of foam, soared
over by screaming gulls. That was Vancouver's English Bay, over
which Catherine now briefly gazed, and on the far side of which, in
the city's West End, she'd long admired a single older apartment
building, white and yellow and stately, far out of her price range but
in which she imagined herself anyway. Kensington Place, it was
called. It was right there on the waterfront on Beach Avenue. She
could dream. And in one of those odd moments of utter stillness amid
dense activity, Catherine's eye was snagged there mid-conversation,
wondering if it was herself she sketched into those wide rooms with
their gleaming hardwood and carved columns, or if she merely
glimpsed another version of herself, existing in parallel. Her but not
her. A theoretical her, possible but only if time could be folded back
onto itself, choices remade, consequences unwound, events respooled.

Yohai was pulling his beard, watching her.

She snapped back. "So . . ." she said. And then she was standing
at the whiteboard squeezed in front of the counter in the kitchen.
She'd drawn a Venn diagram with black marker, three overlapping
circles, one each for *Passion*, *Opportunity* and *Expertise*. The little
space where all three circles overlapped labelled in red: *Sweet Spot*.

No exaggeration. Those first months, that whole first year, they were in a zone where it seemed no new idea did not complete a straight flush. They bootstrapped a prototype for testing. They called it *Red Pill 1.0*. It didn't do any of the diagnostics they were working on beyond blood type and blood pressure. No mooring tech, which was still a long way off. Call it a proto-prototype. But Yohai and Hapok mocked up an application that they loaded up on their phones. Then they all stood around in her living room and they popped those pills, they swallowed them down with tap water. And they waited, staring at their devices. City sounds: sirens, a dog barking, a garbage truck reversing in the alley. Dumpster noise, crashing lids.

Your body is talking. Listen.

Here came the blinking lights, the alerts, phones held out in front of themselves, winking to life with a pulse of music, thrumming bass notes. "Spybreak!" From *The Matrix*. Nice touch.

"Okay, wow," Catherine said, reading her screen. Blood type A positive. Pressure 135/90. High normal.

The boys were high-fiving. *Kicking. Motherfucking. Ass.*

"We could vencap you, like, now." Kalmar talking, a mischievous smile flickering across his features.

She could have stopped it there. *No venture capital. We bootstrap this thing*. She could have turned to Kalmar and said what she'd always believed to be true and told anyone who'd listen. *Investors are Plan Z*.

But she didn't say it because she enjoyed hearing the idea from her own in-house Icelandic metro-mystic. *Vencap you*. She would have been embarrassed for anyone to know the truth: that coming from Kalmar, the words made her proud. And he made it happen too. He knew people, it seemed. So within the month they were in front of their venture capitalist, a man out of Chicago named Morris Parmer. *Wearable diagnostics*, he said on that first occasion of their meeting, high over Randolph and Michigan, expansive views of the lakeshore, the Art Institute, the roll of the horizon where the city's chilling winter winds originated. *Wearable diagnostics is a hell of a growth vertical.*

Catherine didn't typically respond to praise. And she made the right reluctant noises then, gesturing to financials that proved they could see out the year, run version-two tests without additional funding, probably find their way to market with a beta and not need much help at all. During which protestations Morris listened to her alone, not even turning his head when Yohai addressed him, Hapok chiming in now too, each trying to make their separate impressions. Kalmar was silent, but every bit as much ignored.

So perhaps it was in the end simple flattery that held sway in Morris's boardroom as he finally showed the three men the door. *Time for the principals to talk, lads. Coffee? Chai? Drinks?* Catherine was briefly left with the dark wood and the navy patterned carpet. The green-shaded lights. A Remington sculpture on a pedestal in the corner. A cigar box on the sideboard. A long Frank McCarthy original on the facing wall, mounted Cree hunter with cocked bow, raging sea of bison all around him. None of which seemed much like the work Parmer would favour. He was dressed sleekly modern, black crewneck, Apple watch. Silver hair, dark complexion, square features. Sri Lankan, Catherine understood from the bio she'd pulled up online before the meeting. She only knew he seemed more modern than the room somehow, as if it had been put together to impress the Midwestern locals.

Morris came back and gestured for her to take a seat near the window, a light rain rising in the east, scudding clouds, the horizon smudged. Here came a black helicopter in low across the lakeshore, up over Grant Park, climbing the skyways. Catherine saw her face in the glass. And through it, she saw the helicopter wheel up over the river and settle onto the roof of a slender tower, the surface still twenty storeys lower than where she sat, transfixed. The rotors beat the air. Men climbed out—dark suits, briefcases. They made their way ant-like to a doorway, one man holding it open while the other scurried inside. A final look around. The helicopter rising now, feathering down the air, a halo of moisture opening around it. The last man disappeared inside.

Catherine ran him through the basic ideas. She had a vision for something that would change people's lives, their understanding of their own bodies, their engagement with their own health. She had a vision for something that would allow people to take charge of the information their body already possessed. "They say the oceans are the world's biggest remaining mystery," she said to Morris. "I say yes, but it's the ocean within."

Morris, who had sat utterly still listening to her, did not speak immediately now. He looked at her with a serious expression, tempered by some glimmer of recognition, as if she had told him things he'd had occasion to think of in the past, but had perhaps long forgotten in the clamour of life and other concerns. Then, with his hands flat on the mahogany in front of him, he said: "One time in ten thousand an idea walks in those doors with a limitless future and exactly the right person to pursue it."

He said other things. She had worked the miracle, he said. She needed now only the mystery and the juice.

Miracles, mystery and juice. These were the conquering powers, Morris told her. The fuel for a truly Promethean will. These three and you could leave all competition behind.

The miracle was the way you changed the world. "And you've done that already," he said. "You walked in that door with that miracle story. Tell it to people and they will follow you anywhere."

"Juice is money, I take it," Catherine said.

"The resources you gather around you," Morris said. The resources to build and deliver.

"And mystery?" she asked.

There were fathers woven into his answer here. His own and her own. There were families not much talked about. How he even knew that she'd struggled with her father was a mystery to Catherine. Perhaps she glowed with that resentful aura visible to one who clearly bristled at the memory of his own father. In any case, Morris was saying, there were people—entrepreneurs and investors, say—who from their own sides of the table, and each for their own particular and personal reasons, wanted nothing more in business and in life than to go it alone.

"Your pride says a partnership doesn't make sense," Morris said. "Your pride says that accepting my money is giving something away, like throwing yourself into the gorge."

Morris stopped. For effect, clearly, but Catherine did not try to fill the silence. Then he continued.

"But with this deal, Catherine, you'll also make yourself the only one alive who can stop your fall, catch yourself, lift yourself up very high indeed. Think unicorn, Catherine. Think of you riding a unicorn."

The fabled billion-dollar valuation. It was a gauche cliché, and he made that last comment with an invisible but obvious wink.

"What about my social justice causes?" she asked, tone pointed.

A national network of women's shelters, a low-income children's literacy program. Catherine had plans for DIY's success. *Building to flip is building to flop.* They weren't in it to exit. They were in it to enter the community in a meaningful way. They were in it to get people out of walk-in clinics in the Downtown East Sides of the world.

Catherine didn't have much experience pitching the VCs. She had zero experience receiving their pitches. But Morris was in the windup now. And here it came. He'd come in big. She would get her plan financed. She would get her causes. High heat and she caught it clean.

"Separation provision?" she asked.

Very smart to ask, Morris said. *Split pot.* They'd do fifty-fifty on the founders' stake in the company, 51 percent of DIY divided two ways between them. There would be provisions for either of them to walk any time. Let his lawyers work up papers. Say 49 percent held back for stock options and later rounds of investment. It was a good deal, Catherine thought, when she messaged a partner at Phil's firm later that evening. She would have talked to Phil directly, but he was apparently off to Saturna Island again, one of the Southern Gulf Islands off the mainland where he owned a hobby farm. Catherine had occasion to wonder if he sought refuge there and if he did so with anybody in particular.

Parmer Ventures? came the verdict from Phil's partner. *Moneywise there's hardly a decision to make here. Moneywise, you just do the deal.*

What about the buy-sell agreement? Catherine queried. *Isn't that what they call a shotgun clause?*

"We don't really use that term," the partner said, having picked up the phone and called her, clearly concerned she might explode the whole thing at the last second. "Obviously it's up to you. But if you don't sign with Morris you may be wondering for the rest of your life if a shotgun in the hands of a friend is really something to be worried about."

And so came the early money, followed by a tsunami of work sweeping everything away in its path. Catherine rented the warehouse space. They hired. And all the full-stack programmers and developers, all the design people, the social media and market jockeys who came aboard, streaming through the DIY Warehouse, they could all sense it too. The energy of a plan in which people believed. Morris may not have been physically present, but his confidence rang in the white rafters, in the donated artwork from local street artists, in the soundtrack of conversation and keyboards and small tools. Everybody in on the weekends. Everybody working insane hours. Sure, they were paid. But they were also going for something deeper.

She didn't oversell her agenda. It grew in the cracks between people, between ideas, like wild grass, dense with life, energetically green.

Your body. Your data.

And that was no empty offer, either. *The future of medicine*, said the *Mashable* article. *Shirt pocket MD and personal health advisor*, said *WIRED*. Perhaps it was all that too. They had their critics. There were doctors from various quarters taking runs at them. But Kalmar was pulling down research numbers that said the potential market was huge. *People want this. They want this now. If you can have information, why not have it?* They were giving people back a sense of control over something they'd long ago relinquished, control over their own bodies and health, full knowledge of their inner workings and conditions.

They did a market feasibility study through partnership with the University of British Columbia's Sauder School of Business, all lined up by Morris and his connections. They still didn't have the mooring tech down or any diagnostics they could specifically promote, as the development and testing of those remained top secret. But based only on the concept, user response eclipsed expectations anyway. People sensed the potential. Mentions on the tech blogs. Mentions on the local news. They were rising, rising. The Warehouse was hammered. Saturdays. Sundays. Repeat. There was never not a ping-pong game going on. Never not a huddle of people around the whiteboards, process flow charts with data and decision nodes, subroutines and sequences.

Morris was on the phone daily. "Don't worry about what you can't do. Just start building what you can."

"Minimum viable product," Catherine would say. "We are cooking here. You should see this place."

"I'm loving it. I'm loving *this*." And Catherine knew the hand gesture Morris was making, wagging a finger back and forth in the air: *me and you*. "We got this."

They did. Up and up in a single, cresting, exultant wave. There was no sky. Catherine was the sky.

Until she wasn't.

Potential continental partners, Morris said. Of course they'd fly this direction in the new year if he asked them to. But why not send Catherine to them now? A quick trip. She could tell the story far better than Morris. It was hers to tell. He'd booked and paid for a place at Hotel Brighton by the Jardin des Tuileries. Five stars, not exactly the digs to which Catherine had been accustomed. Morris would fly her back through Chicago for a debrief, he told her. Good idea for the two of them to get some face-to-face. He was a kind man in moments like those. He had a team-building character that she knew she lacked herself, always driving things down the lane of her vision, always on her messages. *Make the call, make the decision. Building to flip is building to flop, people.*

Of course all that had worked fine up to a point. Fine and dandy, and she had the sound of ping-pong in her dreams to prove it.

Then AF801 went down and she survived.

The phone had been ringing for a while by the time she noticed. Some strange number, which made her curse aloud. *Damn you. Damn you and whatever you want.* Two years into survival and this was a terrible place to be, hating a phone call when you had no idea if good or bad news was in the offing.

She picked up. She forced herself to speak. She said: "Yes?"

DR. MICHAEL ROSTOCK

HE HAD AN ELEGANT VOICE. "Terribly sorry to bother you. My name is Michael Rostock. Is this Catherine Bach?"

Measured, cautious, considerate yet with determination in reserve. He sounded older.

Catherine listened to the ethereal crackle of phone space for several seconds, a long, steady series of audible breaths signalling that Rostock hadn't rehearsed what came next.

"How did you get this number?" she asked, finally.

"Google, LinkedIn, the National Cellular Directory. It took three minutes, I'm afraid." Rostock's turn to pause. "I'm sorry if . . ."

"What can I do for you, Michael Rostock?" she asked.

Then he came back with it so quickly and firmly that, in a single sentence, he changed from a question to a certainty the most crucial issue of her entire survival. Did she alone obsess about who the others might be, thinking of them, trying to ignore them? Had she alone looked at the seat maps, memorized those magical numbers, recited them in times of distress and anguish?

"Catherine Bach," Rostock said. "You were in 2L, weren't you?"

She couldn't gasp or feel angered at the intrusion. There was no shock. When Rostock said her seat number, she had instead the feeling of something released within. A flutter of wings, briefly agitated, then stilled. A calm descending. It was quite unlike anything she'd felt since before the incident itself. She felt inexplicably and finally safe.

Of course, Catherine did not make a practice of revealing immediately the emotional currents within. So here she registered the feeling: a spreading calmness, the time-lapse shuddering of lake water from ripples to glass in the wake of a breeze. And she did not share a word of it.

Catherine said instead, "And you?"

"70F," he said.

So, Michael Rostock. He gave her the basic details quickly, as if to establish that he was ordinary enough to be trusted. He was a recently retired oncologist, research side. He lived alone in Hyde Park in Chicago, used to work out of the Chicago Comprehensive Cancer Center at the university there, but had also partnered with the Stanford Cancer Institute and Johns Hopkins Hospital. Married twenty-five years. Rostock's wife had died ten years previously of breast cancer.

"I'm sorry about that," Catherine said.

Rostock murmured his thanks and the line ran silent.

"Question?" Catherine said, unsure why on earth this next thing really needed to be asked at all. "Do you still fly?"

He did fly, he told her. He'd never let himself stop. He admitted to a struggle. He'd had all the anxiety that the experts said he was supposed to have.

"You've seen experts," Catherine said.

"Cognitive behavioural therapy," Rostock said. "I did a year or so of that. Cognitive restructuring, stress inoculation training. That and a tapering dosage of benzodiazepine seemed to deal with it."

"And did they help you with the flying?" Catherine asked.

Rostock wasn't sure they had, directly. He'd white-knuckled his first few trips afterwards. Then steadily gotten used to it. "How about you?"

She'd tried three times to buy a ticket, made it as far as the gate and turned around. Not fear exactly, she said. It was a stranger sensation. Like there was something up there she did not feel like meeting again.

Rostock paused on that. She appreciated that he didn't try to complete the package of every idea. "And therapy?" he asked, finally.

She tried but couldn't stay with it, even though the Paxipam prescribed did work to modest effect for sleeping.

"Xanax, for me," he said. "Do you still take it?"

"Oh yeah," she said. "But I've also found pinot noir works if you can hold off until 8:00 p.m. or so."

Rostock's laugh was low and restrained. Like a man who'd laughed more at one time but had grown cautious. "I'll take a gin and tonic on the odd day," he said. "You have to be a bit gentle on yourself. And I didn't go cold turkey on the Xanax either. I tapered off, then quit when the memories became manageable."

He might have been a researcher, Catherine thought, but he had the clinician's touch, gently pointing them back to the central inquiry. So now he was probing, sketching the first moments he remembered himself, a shaking in the fuselage, a shudder then a bang. A sense of falling before the actual start of the descent. Catherine began to cough, a paroxysm of lungs and emotions and the inflamed brain. And she took the phone away from her ear as she did so, staring at it in her hand as if the little wafer with its screen icons might itself be responsible.

Rostock, to his credit, had stopped talking by the time she returned the phone to her ear. He was waiting for her. "Sorry," she said. And so they moved on, having established that she had memories too, probably the same ones. But that they were not going to be discussing them just at that moment.

Rostock changed the subject. DIY. "I've read a bit about the company," he said. "Quite a remarkable thing you're building there."

He knew the story, roughly. High anticipation surrounding the release of the second prototype to test. All the speculation on the DIY blogs. Catherine confirmed what he knew already and then spoke a bit about the germ of the idea. She was still quite capable of remembering what excited her about it, if not always able to fully energize in response.

"They say the biggest remaining mystery on earth is our oceans," Catherine said, repeating a phrase she'd heard herself use often. "I say yes, but it's the ocean of our own bodies."

"Well said," Rostock answered. "And can it really sniff up T-cell counts, liver enzymes, your gizmo?"

"I'll tell you a secret," she said, assuming Rostock was smart enough to know she never actually would. "It's a wearable. But it's also an ingestible."

"Honestly," Rostock said, with a small sigh, "you lost me at *wearable.*"

A whole array of devices that could be placed on or near the body, Catherine explained in brief, fitness trackers and smart watches all deployed with a view to tracking the data available there. DIY just went a little deeper, sending the device inside. You swallowed it.

"And how do you get it to stay inside?" Rostock with that pressing first question.

She deflected. They were still testing that aspect of the technology, but feeling confident.

"Remarkable," Rostock said. And Catherine could hear the next set of questions shaping themselves. She'd had this conversation enough to know what came next with doctors, the concerns about having their own expertise taken out of the loop. The apparent danger of raw, unfiltered data.

"Well, there are health care professionals involved," Catherine said, pre-empting the question. "Data goes to the cloud, where paying subscribers can have their data reviewed."

"And non-subscribers?"

This was the trickiest of her critics' questions. What if someone buys the hardware and swallows this thing, but doesn't pay for the input from experts? There might be liability issues, though DIY lawyers seemed a long way from giving a clear answer on that. Maybe yes, maybe no. Maybe DIY alerts someone to risk factors for kidney disease and they end up taking a toxic dose of milk thistle. Maybe they get sick and someone sues. Maybe.

"It's new territory, not well charted," that particular lawyer had said in a meeting with her and Kalmar a few months back. "But where it gets really interesting is if someone overreacts to an alert that turns out to be false. Guy ODs on some crank remedy to a problem your diagnostics identified, but which autopsy proves was never there at all. Then it's DIY against the aggrieved and we're into complete *terra incognita.*"

"Information wants to be free," Catherine had said then. And she said it again now to Rostock, though feeling measurably less convinced. "I suppose you disapprove. Quite a lot of docs seem to, although plenty of others ask me about buying stock if we go public."

No, no. Rostock laughed his low laugh again. He was fine with the concept, only perhaps because it didn't seem to interfere with his own former area of research. There you'd still need eyes on microscopes, testable hypotheses, blind tests, peer reviews, et cetera.

Catherine took a moment considering an answer, pouring herself a small top-up of wine, wondering if Rostock was perhaps not aware of the latest research in his own field. He was, after all, retired. But before she could even think to speak, he'd moved on.

"But I might approve of your efforts anyway," he said, "just knowing it was you."

Catherine was softened by the comment and thought she understood what it meant. Those few, those lucky or unlucky few. It was an odd bond but a real one nevertheless. And as for him having read a bit about her already, wasn't she just that moment thinking the same thing?

She was walking into the dining room as they spoke, to the table where her notebook was open next to a stack of financial statements and a file of legal correspondence.

"I've read the profile that *Fast Twitch* tried to write," Rostock said.

That would be the profile the tech magazine tried to write without ever getting an interview with her. It was a key disagreement she'd had with Morris that signalled things going sour between them. A year out after AF801. Everything having gone pretty smoothly to that point. She'd actually been quietly pleased at her own resilience, sliding back into the DIY grooves, with so much going on to distract, to deflect negative thought. And progress being made too. Real progress, even if they were behind on the second prototype and an array of niggling problems had been pushing back the test. In the midst of all that, the first anniversary looming and Catherine seeing how it had not really been put that far behind her, how indeed the memories and nightmares had so stubbornly lingered. And Morris chose that moment to decide on her behalf how she should now engage with the world.

"*Fast Twitch*. Tell your story." Catherine couldn't believe it.

"This enormous thing has happened to you," Morris had said to her. "Your survival. We need to work with this story. To talk is healthy."

As if this were about his concern for her personal health. She'd hardly been able to muster a response. And Morris, as if sensing her feelings, then abandoned the health angle and moved on to another, pulling levers, pushing buttons. Hoping against hope that something would work.

"Think of it as outreach. We get people behind the scenes," Morris was saying. Now was the time to do it. Get people into the Warehouse. Let them start to build that relationship. Begin to create that bond.

"Let them see the human faces," Morris was saying. They were more than a company, after all, weren't they? They were Catherine's company.

"Companies don't change your life," Morris said. "People do. You do. So we need your story. The way you *changed your life.*"

Quoting her to herself, drawing on some strategically advantageous moment before. Talking to Morris was on occasion like looking at a YouTube video of some key thing you once said played back through the mouth of what was obviously an evil, manipulative twin.

"Morris, stop," Catherine said. "We aren't selling anything yet. We're still building. We're still testing."

"We are stalling," Morris threw back, putting heat in the friction between them. If they were going to capitalize on early signs of market enthusiasm, Morris went on, they had to test soon and get a beta out there. Test. Then beta. The first prototype had come together so beautifully. What the hell was so different about the second?

So many issues, Catherine explained. Back end, mooring tech, diagnostic modules that needed lengthy testing to get stable data.

"What can it do now, reliably?" Morris asked.

Vital stats, she told him. Heart and respiration rate, blood pressure and glucose levels, body temperature.

Well build that and test it, Morris replied. Curt and sharp. He wanted meaningful results by month end. And there was an oddly punctuating quality to his stress on those words.

Catherine immediately furious. "Since when do I work to your ultimatums?" she asked, a flash of anger passing through her, combined with a veering sense that she did not have complete and typical control over this anger either.

"Everyone works to deadlines," Morris said, his voice now not avuncular at all. "Sometimes people just have to be reminded."

There was a real hardness there. A brittle willingness to fight that she had to assume Morris had always had at his disposal, but that he'd never felt the need to deploy against her before. His lead investment. His darling. Those had been his words.

Well, Catherine thought, two could play at that game, reaching for their tools of conflict at the moment required. So when that smirking young man showed up at the Warehouse on a Tuesday morning just about a year after AF801 went down, Catherine walked him down the street to a dingy pre-Starbucks coffee shop frequented by the trades and the truck drivers so busy in that part of town. The young man's name was Decker and she got him a seat in the swarming room, fetched him a cup of watery joe from the serve-yourself urn on the counter, a Danish so slumped it looked like a failed pancake with a splatter of jam in the middle. Told him to enjoy and that she'd never give an interview she hadn't arranged herself.

He was completely confused, as if he couldn't even understand the words she'd spoken. "People don't generally turn down *Fast Twitch* coverage," he said.

"I'm people," Catherine said. "And this is me turning it down."

"I won't ask personal questions," Decker said, sounding perfectly reasonable. "Just business."

The *Fast Twitch* blog had something like 13 million monthly readers. There was no good reason not to talk to the man about DIY. Catherine knew it as she stood there, as she caught her own reflection in the coffee shop window. She could see herself acting impulsively, emotionally, lecturing the guy about how the vision was hers and hers alone, how she would pursue it, how she would not be broken. *I will not be broken.* And she got quoted saying that too.

Seven emails from Morris the morning after the article ran, which was not a hatchet job exactly but made her sound quotably weird, even in the eccentric world of start-ups. And as his messages arrived that morning, each sounding more hysterical than the last, she wondered at just how significantly the air had now changed

between them. Her vision alone? Morris fumed. Hadn't he been
instrumental in shaping the thing they were doing? Hadn't her carefully chosen and devoted team played some role? If she didn't
appreciate his leadership, if she thought he didn't understand how a
company like this had to be led, if she thought she could be so self-
ish as to keep her story to herself . . .

"Honestly," she told Rostock, "I never even read what *Fast
Twitch* wrote. Someone gave me the gist of it."

And by the time she'd said that, she also had her computer open and
Michael Rostock's name typed in. A few keystrokes and there he was
at the top of the list. Professor Emeritus, University of Chicago at the
Chicago Comprehensive Cancer Center. A few more clicks and she
had his portrait. Sixtyish with silver hair and a square jaw, a proud and
angular nose, narrow smile, a certain sharpness in the creases around
his eyes. Nice-looking man. Handsome even. Tall, she guessed. And
fit. Always wore leather shoes to work, Oxfords or wingtip brogues.

"How do I know this is you?" she asked.

"Well you don't. Which is why I was hoping we could speak in
person." And saying this his voice trailed off in a way that signalled
to Catherine that Rostock himself found it a strange and bold suggestion, and one that Catherine might reasonably decline.

She thought about it, as well as the possibility of simply hanging
up. Easy to do, and she was certain he wouldn't call back. There was
something in his tone, his manner, suggesting that if Dr. Rostock were
refused, he wouldn't press. Yet he was reaching out, this man from
70F, if that's who he really was. And if she wanted to find out whether
he was that man or not, meeting in person was surely the only way.

"Tell me something," she said, leaning back in her chair, staring
out her front window and down Kitsilano Beach, where the waves
were growing blue in the lowering light of evening, and the yellow
accents of Kensington Place on Beach Avenue winked at her across
the water. "Are you in touch with the others?"

"I've been calling around, yes," he said.

So that was his approach, his survival strategy. Catherine couldn't imagine doing the same. Much better to reflect in silence, she thought. Much better to repeat the seat numbers—to be mystified, to wonder without hope of solution—but never know who occupied them. Those lucky few. Let them remain in the shadows, she thought, even while her own horizons had grown cloudy.

"What about you?" Rostock asked.

"No phone calls," she said. "Not for me. But I'm doing all right. I have my days, but I'm basically back on track. True, I don't fly. I get colds a lot, which combined with everything else going on, like psychotic dreams and agoraphobia and a business partner losing his mind now and putting the whole company under unnecessary pressure, just a whole load of bullshit, sorry, that has made things feel a little uphill at the moment. But I'm alive, right? And I see the sun rise and set and I take walks and I believe in what I'm doing. I survived. I'm not lucky. I'm not fated to do great things. I will or I won't be a success here against the same mysterious metrics as everybody else. So I'm happy. I should be happy. I am happy. Really."

Catherine had by this point forgotten what question she was answering and wondered what she thought her falsely brisk tone might communicate. That she didn't feel the weight, the slowing down, the sense of the grade steepening? Maybe she wanted him to believe that, but Rostock wouldn't. Nope, she thought. Dr. Rostock would not buy that story at all. And Catherine had to admit to herself that it was a secret pleasure to realize that. At last, by at least this one person, her bluster would not be believed.

"Listen, Catherine," Rostock said. "More to the point of my call . . ."

And so they came to where they both knew they'd been heading all along, strangers in the midst of their busy, separate lives. Rostock hadn't just called to check on her health, to congratulate her on the success of DIY. His voice was soft at the edges, pulled back. He was himself losing ground in some way. And while they'd said hardly a word about the accident directly, as they'd brushed by the topic of memories earlier, she could not forget the words she had heard, Rostock at the very crest of the fall, trembling in the last seconds of the before. And then the sensations of falling: the feeling of being pressed out, flattened, squeezed in two. Rostock remembered those seconds, he said, as if from within a cloud of sensory nothingness, no smells or sights or sounds to speak of, only that blankness, a white beyond, the idea that he was being driven out of himself and into himself. Separated and co-joined, as if in the same impossible instant.

Catherine listened and wondered briefly. Michael Rostock and Catherine Bach. Had they had exactly the same experience at exactly the same time and in the exact same position above the earth? Did they share something that rare? She wasn't yet entirely sure. But a sliver of uncertainty was perhaps enough for her, for them, hanging as they were in shared phone space, waiting for some final important thing to be said. The real reason he was calling.

He got to that next. The real reason he was calling. He wasn't suggesting they meet just because the conversation might provide comfort, but because he had something urgent to tell her. He would come to her. It was that important.

"I've learned something about what happened to us," Rostock said. "And, Catherine, this is information that you really need. Let me come to you. Let me come to Vancouver. You survived one anniversary of this thing. What I know might help both of us survive many more."

Yet another challenging moment for her. The one course of action was plain. Catherine was by herself in her apartment with a cat she loved, surrounded otherwise by nothing but challenges. A second anniversary approaching and urgent information now struck Catherine as something that she did, in fact, critically need.

The other course of action, simpler, cleaner, altogether more ineffably *her*. Move on, leave well enough alone. And she heard herself answering Rostock to that effect before she might have guessed her brain synapses had even the chance to fire.

iPhone calendar open, ready for her to enter the date.

Then closed. With an electronic winkle, a xylophone trill, a blink of vanishing light.

UNBREAKABLE

SHE DIDN'T CELEBRATE THAT FIRST ANNIVERSARY. You didn't do that kind of thing. You didn't light candles or say prayers, not if you were Catherine Bach. She might have looked over that wrinkled seat plan, traced a finger across the highlighted numbers. Perhaps she even whispered them aloud, though she didn't remember specifically. Year one was passed. *My Annus OK-bilis,* she quipped to Phil. And if the trajectory of things began to bend southwards after the *Fast Twitch* spat with Morris—over the slightly unhinged portrait that the magazine had given of her standing in a coffee shop talking about her vision, about diving the depths of those oceans within—well, then Catherine did not immediately sense it.

They missed Morris's test date ultimatum. The trick was they had to load the device with its diagnostic modules as these came available, which was happening, but not quickly. The diabetes and malaria markers had great data. Most of the others were way behind. Even with those tested, though, they had to get the device to moor properly so that the whole package could be tested over time. Here was the bigger challenge they were as yet failing to meet, a detail Catherine didn't want Morris to know. So she sent him the revised timeline in an email with no reference to mooring, and Morris didn't even bother responding.

He was in Thailand, she heard. Investing in something there. She hoped it would distract him.

Of course, she didn't tell Rostock any of these year one details. She didn't ask him how he might have celebrated surviving that year, or if after doing so he'd begun to see an incremental lengthening of the shadows. She didn't tell him how after the anniversary, after that article ran, her cred with the geeks and the code-jockeys seemed even to lift a little. Sideways glances from those privately impressed with her poor media skills, her in-print weirdness. *I will not be broken.*

She should have seen it coming. *Unbreakable* read the title on the repurposed movie poster that was hung over her workstation one Monday morning, Bruce Willis's face skilfully Photoshopped out and her own half-shadowed image ghosted in. In the weeks after the crash itself, she guessed no one would have dared. One year later, even AF801 was fair game.

"There are two reasons why I'm looking at you like this."

Some wag from the back-end group. He was a database expert. He was a coder. He was a classic geek bro with his peach fuzz beard, aviator-frame glasses, untucked shirt from The Gap, bright red. He was what, twenty-three, twenty-four years old? Catherine couldn't remember his name. Grady. Justin. But there he stood at the edge of her workstation. She could feel the others watching from the across the way.

She looked at him with a weary smile, decided his name was Yukihiro even though he didn't look Japanese because it was the kind of name his parents might well have given him, and for that matter maybe he was Japanese.

"One," he said. "Because it seems in a few minutes you will officially be the only survivor of this train wreck."

Long pause. Giggling in the background.

"And two: because you don't have a scratch on you."

Catherine sighed, still looking up. Same smile, unamused but tolerant. "But I did get scratched, genius," she said. "If you're going to quote the movie, at least pick a line that fits."

They laughed, those watching. And the database boy went back to his work with a backwards grin. Which Catherine returned, because you had to play nice even if the humour was mixed with a portion of garden-variety code-jockey chauvinism. Some kid just out of school making good money with the promise of stock options, testing the woman in charge. A woman in charge, imagine that.

Catherine thought simply, *Well, I am in charge. I am* still *in charge. So eat my shorts.*

"Need anything, Red? Let me get you something." Kalmar now, who had an uncanny ability to read her emanations and had acquired the knack of stepping in to divert her darker moods. There he was just at the safe edge of her work zone, a hand to the edge of her desk, his fingernail touching the wood, those ice-blue eyes on her and holding her.

I'm good. She told Kalmar so, offhand and with brightly false good humour. *All good, Kali. All good.* And off he went, back to work, no backwards glance. She watched him prowl away and off up between the work benches, people bent to their various tasks, stuffed animals in the rafters. Kali working his way across to the far wall where he'd set up his own station, and she caught him from time to time looking towards the window, low light lying full on his features. He'd come back later for a visit, she knew. He'd bring her a coffee or some popcorn or a Clif Bar. She wondered vaguely if the time might come when she'd have to stop the practice, office politics being what they were, perceptions of favourites, petty jealousies. But she pushed her mind off the topic, hating to think any change would ever be necessary.

So began year two, feeling still okay. Catherine striding into the Warehouse past the bike racks. There were energized meetings in progress, whiteboards scrawled with optimism. There were people hunched at their workstations, gathered in groups at the clustered chairs and tables. There were people standing in the kitchen and dining zone, the ping-pong table, the wooden teepee in the centre of it all, soundproofed, where teleconferences were hosted or you could just go for peace, or to exchange words in private, make out illicitly with a colleague. Who thought of installing the teepee? Catherine didn't know. A designer, one assumed. And Catherine didn't want to know everything that the designers did or thought, or what went on in the teepee or even at every workstation. She wanted to trust people to their individual parts of the greater thing that she was envisioning and building. *Change your world.* She'd keep an eye on the big picture and let people do their jobs. She was still the field marshal, alone on the ridge line. And yes, as in virtually all tech settings, she was surrounded by men. Lads and brothers and bros who just had a certain way of living with each other. Like combat robots, she thought, always taking runs at each other, hacks and tricks, porn screensavers installed on a colleague's system. They never involved her in any of it. They had ways of letting her know she stood apart, hanging their '70s repro posters of Farrah Fawcett and Cheryl Tiegs, tuning the Warehouse jukebox in to old metal and hip hop, Iron Maiden, Metallica, once the Beastie Boys' "Hey Ladies" on repeat until Catherine herself went over and pulled the plug.

And did her management team always rise above it? Kali, Hapok, old friend Yohai? They did not. Not before the accident. And certainly not a year after. But she let them all just be who they were, do what they did. And they seemed to like her for it. Year two had not yet begun to punish her in those first months, not in ways that she could actually measure.

So why agree to see a therapist? She wondered now about that detail, if talking about things had nudged events into negative motion. Maybe she shouldn't have listened to Phil on that one.

"Is it about that stupid article?" she asked him, when he brought it up.

He laughed. "Of course not."

"What then? Something Morris said. We've had delays. I'm aware of that."

Nothing like that. This was a friend talking, he reminded her. And it was her friend who'd noticed her increasing distraction. It was her friend who'd noticed her getting behind on things.

"And it's me, your friend, saying that I saw you sitting in the car outside before coming into the café just now," Phil said. "It was me who saw you crying."

Phil was looking at her, eyes concerned but kind.

"Was I . . . ?" she started. She had a hand on her face, on her cheek, as if to find evidence of tears.

"I believe in experts," Phil said. "I believe in finding the specific ones you need in specific moments. It's no shame. It's just smart."

There had to be someone in your life whose advice you really took seriously. So she went. She said: "This is my lawyer's idea. He's super-smart, though I'm not sure what he knows about therapy since I don't think he's ever done it himself."

Catherine twisting her hands into nervous knots, squirming on the leather Corbusier chair in the therapist's office up on Lonsdale Avenue in North Vancouver.

"Maybe he's never needed one," said the therapist, a psychologist originally from Ecuador, with three PhDs judging from the certificates on her office wall. Ximena Briana Diaz. Absolutely Latin gorgeous, Catherine thought. And the faint trace of moustache did nothing to detract.

"Probably not," Catherine said, shredding a Kleenex now, hands tremoring. "But what about me? Do I need to be here? I ask in the means-tested sense of it. Am I typical of the kind of person you'd see?"

"How long has it been?"

A year, Catherine told her. Well, more now. God, time was really flying. Fourteen months. No, she'd never sought help previously. In the immediate aftermath it hadn't seemed necessary.

"Do you still have bad dreams?" Ximena's voice was capable of a pragmatic hardness. She had not been coddled in life. And even the plants in her office seemed to advertise this: a ball cactus, a mescal agave plant, a Manua Loa succulent. These things made rocks their home.

"Do you still startle when people approach you from behind? Are you scared in elevators? Do you feel grief and guilt at the same time? This feeling of grieving at the exact same time that you are feeling that you have no right to grieve?"

Ximena had a photo on her desk of a man Catherine presumed was her husband. He stood in a wool sweater on the deck of a ship, Vancouver's inner harbour over his shoulder. Tugboat captain, Catherine mused. How romantic was that? Wool sweater, black watch cap, a Band-Aid across one knuckle. But admiring the sureness evident in the man's expression, and what that implied about Ximena's own life, only drove Catherine to consider how sureness had been draining from her own. The point was precisely that in the immediate aftermath she hadn't felt very much of any of the things Ximena had mentioned, the startling, the claustrophobia, the toxic duality of grief and guilt. They'd only started to crop up later, growing, organic things somehow spreading in her with every nightmare, every glimpse in peripheral vision of some dark gathering there at life's fringes. And Catherine found a panic rising in her chest as she thought that through, at the same time registering with sudden and painful clarity all the real-world work that still had to be done in the face of these inner realities. They were finally in test on the mooring tech. She needed to contact the lab. She needed to talk to the technicians there. She needed to talk to Yohai about device tolerances and about whether or not they knew yet definitively that stomach acid concentration variances would or would not affect device transmission rates in certain circumstances. A lot was riding on factors like this one and dozens of others. The *Red Pill 2.0* completion dates. The beta test. The rollout that Morris had been pushing them towards, pushing and pushing.

Ximena was still talking. Catherine herself had been talking, answering questions she did not remember. Fielding another one, just now.

"Do you ever find yourself crying without having felt the tears on the way?"

Catherine was biting her fingernails. And given the tears that were appearing on them, she knew that she was now crying too. *Like now?* she wanted to ask, but somehow could not speak the words. *You mean like what's happening to me right now?*

She never told Phil when she stopped going. Catherine didn't think he'd disapprove exactly. Phil didn't really do disapproval. But he might think quietly less of her for being insufficiently clear-minded to accept professional advice. Too high-strung to analyze. Too emotional to pay for help.

But then, muted disapproval and worrying were always more jobs for sisters. And Valerie had been registering her worry lately. She was calling more, suggesting coffee dates, suggesting Catherine come over for movie nights with her two sweet kids. She owned an antique shop in West Vancouver's Ambleside Village that she populated with textiles and dishes, handmade candles, old apothecary bottles and ivory-handled cutlery that she found on her trips to France, or that her network of buyers otherwise sourced. She was good at finding things. Catherine could never really picture the houses and lives into which these objects fit. But Valerie Bach Design was a thing now, apparently. She was doing remarkably well. And she seemed happy, too, married to a guy who ran an ethical green-energy mutual fund. Mark, whom Catherine felt guilty for finding incredibly boring. How different their lives had always been. And in the moments Catherine thought about that—approximately every time she'd been in Valerie's shop or home—she would also invariably remember their own lawyer father and his chauvinist ideas about women's careers. Their mother, she of the original flowing red locks, suffered in silence her entire foreshortened life. Catherine had always been the one to argue, to fight and rail against her father's various oppressions, may he of course also rest in peace. But Valerie had been the pleaser, the striver, smarter than Catherine almost certainly, but destined somehow to sell beautiful things to beautiful women with lives much like Valerie's own.

"The rational fact of it is that you can't really *work* on the past," Catherine said to her sister, when the abandoned therapy finally came up a month after she'd quit. That's what they said: *work on it*. But by definition, it was in the past. It was a previously sampled data set. It was beyond working, beyond being changed. So why even talk about it?

Valerie didn't think that Catherine quite understood what talk therapy was supposed to be about, but she was gentle saying so. Sometimes people worked on their feelings about the past, she said. They changed their relationship to the past. They changed the way they reflected on or possibly fixated on the past.

"Like I'm fixated?" Catherine said.

"No, no, no. Well a bit," Valerie said.

"I'm healthy!" Catherine said. "I'm really good. I did yoga yesterday."

Which was a flat-out lie. She had not even contemplated doing yoga. And since when did she lie to her sister?

"Well if you ever want to talk to me . . ."

"I'm so good," Catherine said again. And her sister pretended to believe her. Pretended to be unconcerned. Pretended that the dinner party she and Mark were hosting over the weekend would be something Catherine might actually attend and that she would not come up with last-minute excuses. But of course Catherine knew all along that she would. She could see herself on Saturday night and she knew where she'd be. She'd be at the Warehouse in front of a screen. She'd be reviewing data from the lab or from Hapok on the site or from Kali on the market view.

And that's exactly where she was then. On that Saturday. On the following Saturday. On a string of Saturdays that grew and grew to the point that one Saturday she experienced a deeply strange sensation, which shaped itself in the air around her like a vision: a fractured view of her own profile, in place across all those Saturday nights stretching into the future. Repeating and repeating and repeating.

Yohai was there, he was on the other side of the desk. He'd come over to talk with her about the reports that had just come in from the lab. And she knew from the arrangement of his features that he was about to give her bad news, but she found herself unable to quite hear him speaking, awash as she was suddenly with that flickering vision of herself in place on multiple days, in multiple moments. And as she sat there, more or less frozen, a chilling interpretation of the experience suddenly came to her, the sense of those future iterations of her body not quite being her own, that in that moment she was seeing some other version of herself alive in the world.

Someone turned on the jukebox, just then. Beck. De La Soul. Run-DMC. One of those.

Here it comes, Catherine thought. And she seemed to blink awake. She caught herself there and returned to the person that she understood people needed her to be.

"Say again, everything that came after hello," she said, back in a sheering dive from the ether of visions and into her own chair.

The device had failed to moor, Yohai was explaining. The lab had been feeding dummy Red Pills for two months to a chimpanzee named Mickey who was unharmed by the experience, but whose stomach was not letting the tiny device remain *in situ* as was required.

Catherine paused and sat back. She chewed her lip.

"I hate to say I told you so," Yohai said.

"Don't then," Catherine said. "Ideas would be better."

"We go subcutaneous."

Catherine dropped her head to the desk, forehead down. "Not this," she said.

"The device is good. We know it works. We're loading the diagnostics as they come online. Where we park it is the outstanding question, and subcutaneous is known and tested."

"We're not giving up on ingestible."

"Let's talk to Morris," Yohai said.

"Fuck that," Catherine said, and heard her words echo in the rafters above, refract through the dust motes floating there.

"Whoa," Yohai said. "I'm just saying get his opinion."

"We tell no one," Catherine said.

"What is this then? What are we doing?"

"We're tweaking the formula," she said. "We're testing again."

"We're nowhere near a real full feature test," Yohai said. "Because we're hung up on this one feature that we could work around."

"I'm not going to market with an idea that requires people to have surgery," Catherine said. "That's just sending them back to the doctors we're supposed to be helping avoid."

"You say surgery like it's an organ transplant," Yohai said.

"It's a matter of principle," Catherine said. "We're promising people control."

"We're talking about a routine procedure with a local anesthetic," Yohai said. "You're on the street in five minutes and back in control."

"We're going to make this work!" Catherine said, voice raised.

"Our timetables are going into serious skew here, Cate," Yohai said. And now his voice was up in volume also. "Device functions are coming together. We're getting stable data on a good range of diagnostic modules. Hapok is building out the site. Kalmar is kicking motherfucking ass out there on the user side. We have pre-regs like crazy. Where we're hurting is delivering an actually testable product. Where we're hurting is right here."

He meant her. She knew it and it made her furious. But she did not budge. And she did not ask a second time. Yohai had his orders and he would follow them through. They would make the mooring tech work. Meanwhile, she would hide anxiety. She would not let them know. Not Kalmar, who still brought her snacks in the afternoon when she was looking like she could use it. Who did not know anything about the mooring tech, but who did not ask unwelcome questions about the schedule either, even as the months stretched. He seemed to keep his faith, perhaps even strengthen in it, while she struggled herself with darker thoughts of betrayal. Of Morris in the wings. Of Yohai's fragile loyalty. Of falling and falling and falling.

"Your bones don't break, mine do." Kalmar at her desk, but with a smile she understood. He had in his hands a hot bowl of kimchi ramen from the kitchen. He had the chopsticks. He had the packet of extra soy and the shaker of shichimi peppers he knew she liked.

She took the bowl in her hands. She lowered it to the desk between her and the keyboard. She looked up at him. "Kali," she said, her voice quiet.

He waited. Head just a bit to one side.

"Would you stop with that whole *Unbreakable* thing, Kali, please? It feels old. I took the poster down months ago."

He smiled. Of course he would stop. She knew he would.

"Thanks for this," Catherine said, straightening up in her chair. "Thanks generally."

"*Nei*," Kalmar said. "*Takk fyrir.*"

"You going to teach me some of that one day?" she asked him. "Icelandic?"

"Any time," he said. "What do you want to say?"

"Good swears?" she answered, picking up the chopsticks.

"Ah," he said. "Well we can probably do better than that."

Off he went. A flash of blue eyes and a smile. Then he was walking away in his characteristic fashion, no glance back, a word with the lads as he passed, only this time walking all the way across the Warehouse, past the teepee and on to the bikes where he found his own old road bike—chipped paint, warped leather seat, all the handlebar wrapping long gone—and pushed it on out the door and into the sunshine. He could go, of course. He was himself admirably under control, in his work at DIY and seemingly in everything else too. Catherine watched him and felt, herself, only the fractures within. The setback and the mounting fear. And she would not dream of Kalmar later either, three in the morning in twisted sheets. Again and again, mounting in intensity: water and fire and the blackest birds. She swam in those images, the dense cold and the searing heat, the feathery black shroud. And when she awoke she was drenched in sweat, trembling, spilling the bedside glass of water on the hardwood floor, glass breaking. Catherine cursing at three o'clock in the morning at herself and this highly breakable thing that she had become.

And then, the leak.

Was that the factor that finally changed things forever? Someone broke confidence. Someone broke ranks. Someone broke the code. Eighteen months out from AF801. Catherine remembered going to sleep the night before thinking of the now seemingly distant anniversary, wondering with dark seriousness if she had the stamina to make a second. Terrible sleep that night. The usual terrible dreams. But she woke with an unusual, trembling type of energy. Woke and piled out of bed into unwashed clothes, headed in to work only to stop at a café not far from the Warehouse. She'd driven in but could not quite let herself arrive. She'd stopped short, gone to caffeinate. Sitting at a side table with a matcha tea, surfing the news and there it was: the skunkworks projects weren't so secret any more. It was all over everywhere. They'd made *Gizmodo*. They'd made *ZDNet*. They'd made *WIRED* and *Mashable*. *Red Pill 2.0* would have a serious payload if it was ever delivered and managed to stay in place. And there it all was in clickable black and blue and white: tumour markers, pre-cancerous tissue detection, early alerts on diseases mundane and exotic. Her own plans for the company too, her own more personal visions. Social justice causes. Everybody seemed to know everything. Not the working details, clearly. Nobody was that stupid. She had the information mapped down to the person, who knew what and when they knew.

"This is a fucking leak."

Catherine in a rage. An intern stood at the foot of the picnic table where they were meeting, tears brimming. She had nothing to do with anything. She'd just brought over coffee from the canteen and got caught in the crossfire.

Yohai, trembling with indignation. Hapok looking distant, hand stroking his dog's golden head. Kalmar brooding for his part, tip of his handsome chin balanced on one fist.

"Talk to me," Catherine said. "Talk to me now. How would they know we're working with the TRIUMF collider on tissue markers? Tissue markers are a new, new thing. TRIUMF doesn't talk about it. We don't. Or we didn't. Kali, you're supposed to be market-facing. What the honest fuck?"

He looked at her, beautiful eyes now sorrowful, the light blue carrying the trace of a deeper colour. He spread his hands. "I come in. I work with my team. I build this thing. I don't talk to other people. I don't know any other people."

Hapok's eyes had drifted to the window. Like this meeting didn't concern the website boys. She turned on him, let him have it. What did he think a designer was supposed to be doing? Design, goddamn it. Design things.

"Like I didn't just build a beta website three and half million people still don't have a reason to use," Hapok said.

The beta website was a piece of shit, Catherine said. Why was she clicking around in there drowning in a sea of pages explaining the physiology of a melanoma tumour?

"We talked about a symptom wiki, Catherine," he said. "So we're just doing what designers do. We're designing stuff. We were just glad to have a clear decision for once."

"What does that mean?" she said. But she knew. Slow answers to emails. A creeping incremental stasis, moments where she caught herself in a stupor at her desk, stupors the length of which she could not always remember.

The wiki was a dumb idea, even if it had been hers. The Red Pill was supposed to read the symptoms so you didn't have to. A wiki was completely redundant. What was everybody doing? Who was talking to who?

Hapok had stopped arguing by that point. But there was now the flickering light of real confusion in his eyes. She wasn't scanning right to any of them, she could sense. Not even Kalmar, who Catherine thought instinctively knew her better than the others. Understood her with very few words. He was now staring at the table in front of himself, leaving her alone with his eyes. His deference sobering her suddenly, causing her to sit down having just then realized she'd been standing, pacing back and forth in front of the window, the morning sunshine streaming in behind her, blinding everyone else in the room.

"Hey, listen," Catherine said to the intern, who was still fighting tears. "This is not you. Thanks for the coffee. You're good."

Yohai came and found her later out behind the Warehouse. Catherine was standing next to a dumpster and staring up towards the distant, north shore hills. His manner reflected a simmering concern, but no combativeness. He wasn't there to argue. He stood next to her, said nothing, followed her gaze.

"That's the thing with mountains," he said, finally. "You have to watch them every second."

Catherine sighed. "I'm turning into an unpredictable bitch."

Yohai shook his head. "Nah," he said. "Listen, though. You gotta appreciate we're all on your side."

Catherine nodded, turned back to the mountains, gazing up. "See up there?" she said.

Yohai followed her gaze again. He looked up at the mountains.

"When I was a kid, I had an angel up there."

Yohai was now quiet beside her.

"It was a pattern of snow in the hills there, just west of the Lions." She held out a finger and pointed to where the mark of a clear-cut had left the shape of a wing. She could tell that Yohai wasn't seeing it. But Catherine could still easily make it out, despite the lack of snow to fill in its lines: the reclining head, the spreading wings, two little feet poking up.

Yohai cleared his throat. "Morris called me just now," he said. "Wondered why you weren't answering your phone."

"He was the leak, wasn't he?"

"You could make a case that he has the most to gain." Yohai twisting a blade of grass between his fingers. "Of course you could make a case that you do too."

Catherine looked over at him. His eyebrows were squinted behind those steel frames. He was still staring up at the mountain, perhaps still wondering where exactly that angel might be.

"The more hype, the more valuable your respective shares," he said.

"I get it," she said. "But you know I wouldn't do that."

Yohai sighed. "I do know that, yes. I also know that it wasn't Morris."

"Know how?"

"Because he's a pro."

"Maybe this is what pros do."

"Because I just talked to him and asked him and he said no. Because I judge him to be telling the truth."

Catherine shook her head. "So the competition now knows exactly what we're doing. I say we write a press release and deny it all."

"But some of it's true," Yohai said. "All of it's true."

"We deny it anyway," Catherine said. "Then when we go to market, we say those features came later."

"That is a really bad idea," Yohai said. "You want to release *negative information* about the company when we're in the chute, trying to finish testing and get a beta out?"

Catherine crossed her arms and looked away. He was sickeningly right.

"We're way out in front, Cate. We have patents. We have the device, the power source. We don't have our mooring tech. But we'll figure that out somehow. And you still have this team."

"Thanks for that," she said. "But Morris signed a non-disclosure."

"I said I don't think it was him."

"Since when are you and Morris so chummy?" Catherine asked.

"Ah, man," Yohai said. "So what? You sue? Trigger the shotgun clause and buy him out?"

"Is that so crazy?" she demanded. She turned on Yohai more squarely now. In the breeze there were traces of the sea. There were trees, pavement, fumes and the lower scent of swirling ideas.

"Maybe not crazy," Yohai said. "But doing that just got a helluva lot more expensive."

Right, Catherine thought. Of course. Speculation. Increased market values. Morris didn't have to actually pick up the phone and call people. Maybe he'd only seeded the rumour somewhere he knew it would leak from. An arm's-length colleague. A buddy at the club. However he did it, and for whatever reason, Morris did have an interest in boxing her out. He had the deep pockets. He had the resources. He also knew that she didn't.

"Are you all right?" Yohai said, reaching out a hand to touch her shoulder, Catherine just that moment realizing she was hunched over, hands pressed to her face, blotting out the light and sound.

She straightened up. She shook off Yohai's hand. And she turned back to the mountains. No particular inspiration arriving, just looking up to her faded angel. It had been Valerie who'd first seen it, pointed it out, gesturing and explaining. For a long time Catherine couldn't make it out. Then, even after Valerie seemed to have forgotten about it entirely, the angel came sharply into focus, where it had since remained.

Catherine's phone was ringing again. Ringing and ringing. Both she and Yohai could hear it. No point pretending to ignore.

"Well I guess I'll let you take that," Yohai said.

Catherine watched him retreat, down the side of the Warehouse, then around the corner and out of sight. And later, when she thought back on that moment, Catherine couldn't remember taking the phone call. Couldn't remember who it had been calling just that moment as she gazed up at her angel and Yohai left her alone. It could have been the lab, which had gone back to working those tests. It could have been Phil, or Morris himself. Valerie. It could have been any number of people bearing the incrementally worsening news. *That slow wrong turning.*

Catherine remembered only the birds on the wires of the power poles opposite. Every tiny black head seeming to cant to one side at once, beaks elevated, as if the birds were in one gesture, as one entity, closely listening to her.

Back to her desk, still later. It was just what you had to do. Back to the workstation, chair swivelled around to the window. She began to write the press release that would almost certainly make everything worse. She wrote the whole thing out. Loaded up an email to Decker from *Fast Twitch*. Might as well put those bastards to work. The device did not do what people were saying it did.

Then she deleted it and she sat with her eyes on the window. Out there: railway sidings growing over with tall weeds, the brick perimeter walls, leaning and cracked and covered in graffiti, mountains and rising blue sky flecked with cirrus clouds. In here: Catherine's own hands trembling in her lap, fingers laced together as if in prayer. Phones ringing and people trotting past her workstation. Andy, Codette, Ruger, Stitch. A kid with a beard she didn't recognize. Another intern, this one brought in only the day before, whose name was Arwen, whose parents had actually named her after an elf in *Lord of the Rings*. Her own desk stacked with files and forms to sign. Letters from lawyers. A folder of financial statements from the accountant. It would all go on well enough without her, when Morris got his way. Catherine was momentarily convinced of that, at least. Everything would continue just fine. And if there was some pride to be taken from having built the business, maybe that was just it: knowing that the machinery would keep turning over even after you were chased from the premises.

She wasn't crying again, Catherine told herself, she was just blowing her nose. She was stuffed up. Her eyes were running. She was eighteen months older than she'd been when AF801 went down. And she thought of those seat numbers then, for the first time in weeks. She wondered at them and who they were. She wondered how they each had been doing, each, she assumed, in the funnel of their own struggles and mounting frustrations. Things gone strange. And thinking this, Catherine reached unconsciously, automatically for a lower desk drawer and opened it. Xanax, Klonopin, Paxipam, Valium, Ativan. Her doctor had recently told her: listen, if you want to try different ones, be my guest. You're a grown woman and I'm sure you know not to do any two at the same time. Or with alcohol.

Or swallow an entire bottle, Catherine thought. He hadn't said that, but it was the implication. Don't just go to sleep forever to escape the mounting messiness of life around you.

She got up again, agitated. But she did not walk outside. She stood near the window and looked at the point in the mountain that was the farthest away. Her angel was invisible to the west, so it was the tip of Grouse Mountain instead. She stared and felt the muscles around her eyes readjust, stretch. Relax.

She would not swallow the entire bottle of anything. At the very least, she would not do that yet. And since Catherine knew she wouldn't be having a glass of wine until much later that evening, she chose the Klonopin, just the one tablet, and slid shut the drawer.

"HOW LONG HAS IT BEEN SINCE THE ACCIDENT?" Ximena asked her.

"Coming up on two years," Catherine said.

"And the other time I saw you?" There was no judgment here. Catherine was looking at the pictures on the therapist's desk again, the degrees on her wall. Ximena crossed her legs, waiting. She was wearing gorgeous boots today, Catherine couldn't help but notice. Soft black leather, riding heels. Ximena on a horse was very easy to visualize, her back ramrod straight, hands lightly and authoritatively on the reins.

"Six months? Eight?" Catherine said with a sigh. "I came that first time on my lawyer's advice."

"Philip," said Ximena.

Catherine was surprised, not recalling that Phil had been discussed. "Yes," she said.

"Divorced. Lives in a big house in West Vancouver." Ximena was apparently reading notes. She glanced up now and looked at Catherine steadily. "And so why try this time?"

Where to start? Catherine thought. Worsening nightmares. Worsening daymares. All of the men in her life seeming to have their separate demands. Then of course this Dr. Rostock phoning out of the blue. Each of those would probably be worth a session for the kind of people who did therapy. But Catherine only squirmed in place, twisting in that black leather chair, nervous and uncertain, passing a take-away coffee cup back and forth between her hands.

Ximena was looking at her notebook, scribbling something in the margin. She said, "Let's start with the men at work."

Catherine sighed.

"This Morris," Ximena said with a frown. "Are you still angry with him?"

So they'd talked about Morris already too. All right. Well. "He leaked confidential information about our product to the press," Catherine said. "That breaches his NDA. And it pissed me off, yes."

Ximena looked up. "You're sure it was him?"

Yohai might think otherwise, but Catherine was sure. Who else had a motive? Morris, on the other hand, had many. But inflating the company's value in advance of product release was a good guess. Maybe he was setting himself up to sell his share.

"Maybe he just wants to destabilize me," Catherine said. "Push me out."

Ximena waited. Catherine's eyes went to the window. They were doing sewer work in the avenue below. Men in orange vests standing with shovels, staring into a hole. They seemed transfixed by something in the darkness down there.

"He also started showing up in Vancouver unannounced."

Catherine had been in the thick of things. After the leak, Morris had taken a much higher-profile role in day-to-day decisions. He claimed that it was his concern about the leak that drove his involvement, a high irony in Catherine's mind. But there he was, phoning in to meetings he'd never bothered with before. Phoning Yohai and Hapok directly with questions, which was infuriating because it made miscommunication more likely. His own emails to Catherine grew much more frequent and on some days seemed to arrive at unusually late hours. That last detail caught her one night in particular. Catherine in bed reading Mary Shelley's *Frankenstein*, skimming pages, more or less reminding herself how the story worked against some vague and yet compelling logic that the reminder was necessary—and it suddenly occurred to her that if Morris was emailing her, he was up at two in the morning Chicago time.

Where are you? she wrote back.

In Vancouver, he admitted.

"And this concerned you?" Ximena asked.

"Because I knew why he was here."

The week before he'd asked to review all the mooring tests from the lab. Catherine hadn't even told him how the technology worked, and she didn't particularly feel like telling him now because he didn't need to know, because it was hard to explain, and because he'd probably just leak that too. So she'd been not answering his request on that one, and he'd gone and asked Yohai, who didn't know any better and coughed up the name of the procedure.

"What is *plasma membrane transformation*?"

That was Morris on the phone, sounding suspicious.

She gave him the dumbed-down venture capitalist version, the one least likely to freak him out. Basically it was a process where you made the device sticky once it interacted with stomach acid. That allowed the device to gently adhere to the stomach wall and stay in place to provide diagnostic feedback over the longer term, which was, she reminded Morris, a key DIY value proposition.

"All right," Morris said. "So when are we going to lock that in and go to beta?"

Well not quite yet. It was just a question of getting the triggering elements in the coating correct so that the reaction reliably occurred and didn't undo itself in a few days.

Morris sighed impatiently. And what exactly was *hyperlocalized endometrialization*?

Yohai and his big mouth, she thought.

With Morris, she just told him it was technical. There were proteins and nucleic acids involved. Hormonal activators. Bottom line, by interacting with the stomach wall, the device induced the cells it contacted to act like magnets. The device attached to those cells. It didn't interrupt digestion. It was imperceptible to the host. They'd modelled it in computer simulations. Only they were struggling to make it bond firmly in the animal trials.

Endometrialization. Ximena was nodding. "You're getting people pregnant."

"Well, no," Catherine said. "The device implants. But nothing grows. It just sits there and transmits. Ideally it stays for a year before the battery dies, then the device de-endometrializes and is naturally evacuated."

"So did you see Morris on any of his visits here?" Ximena asked.

Catherine sighed and put her face in her hands.

Morris was visiting to see the lab where they were testing the mooring tech, Catherine felt sure. He was going to snoop around there and tear apart those test results, maybe try to come up with something to discredit her. That was Catherine's best guess at the time. She called over to the lab the next day and talked to the woman she worked with most closely there, a molecular biologist, Dr. Ophelia Burke. Dr. Burke hadn't heard from anyone named Morris and sounded confused by the question. And then she was also distracted with recent developments: the latest tests were showing greatly improved results.

"I think we've got a three-month formula," Burke told Catherine.

A device that could stay moored for three months was indeed good news. It wasn't a full year, which had been Catherine's firm target, a real fire-and-forget type of device that could help people over the long term without surgery, without scars. But three months was certainly better than three days, their previous best result.

Catherine elected not to tell Morris that. At three months he would force the prototype into test, something she did not yet want to do. And for his part, Morris had gone oddly quiet after their last conversation. Catherine almost managed to forget about him for a while, as the team was still dealing with challenges across virtually all parts of the platform. They had glitches in the cloud analytics. They had a bug in the customer database that was deleting pre-registered accounts. They had liability and scaling questions pressing and unresolved.

So Catherine was busy. But there had been one evening, on Kalmar's quiet and persuasive suggestion, that she did head home on the early side, just after 6:00 p.m., to take a bit of a breath, to walk the seawall, through Kitsilano Park, then up the hill along Yew Street, past the restaurants there. And halfway up the hill, winded from the climb, she stopped to turn around and look back at the sea, and there was Morris.

Morris and a woman, sitting in a restaurant called Look Homeward Angel.

They were at a table not far from the window. And while the deepening blue on the sidewalk outside rendered Catherine invisible, the light inside revealed the woman plainly and made Morris's expressions easy to read. So she stood and stared, and thought that sometimes the way people arranged themselves in conversation didn't need to be explained. Sometimes it was obvious. And here you had an obvious example of co-conspirators.

Morris canted forward, eyes hooded and dark. The woman with her head to one side, clearly listening. Then replying with a nod and a finger raised and pointed. An idea being shared. A cunning scheme taking shape as Morris sat back and put a fist on the table, nodding in agreement. Nodding at some sort of commitment to plan.

The woman was quite notably blond. Catherine had met Dr. Ophelia Burke only once. But she too had that Nordic colouring. And now the woman was laughing. Catherine could tell from the way her head leaned back and the way those blond coils shook. She could tell from the way Morris looked so pleased, having said just the right thing for the moment.

Catherine was inside the restaurant's front door by that point, she realized suddenly, in that shuddering way that she had lately found herself blinking awake in just a slightly different place and posture than she last remembered occupying. It was as if she appeared in her own peripheral vision, seeing herself but not herself, only then to sharply reanimate in her new position. She had stepped from behind the pony wall, from behind the ferns. She had advanced some distance down the aisle between the door and Morris's table. And Morris, of course, because it was just that kind of waking anxiety dream—another shuddering movement at the edge of her field of view, another sharp realignment of her place in the room—had seen her and raised a hand in greeting, and the woman had turned around to see who he was greeting. And she was not blond at all.

Morris called to Catherine as she turned and rushed the other way, out the front door, onto the sidewalk. He struggled to his feet, sliding out past the tables, following her. *Catherine?*

On the sidewalk there were confused words. Morris reaching out to take her shoulder. She didn't slap him, though that now seemed insanely near the top of her list of options. But she roughly shook off his hand and fled, humiliated and not even entirely certain why. Catherine running down the hill into the safety of the blackness there. Into the park and across it through the comfort of those silent trees.

"So that was Morris destabilizing you," Ximena said, finally. "Trying to push you out."

Catherine wouldn't have expected a therapist to deal in irony. But then, it had been a ridiculous moment.

Morris, for his part, tried to be easygoing about the strange encounter, though they both knew that it had been strange. The woman was his cousin, he told Catherine, during which phone call she also learned that he'd be staying a few more days. Catherine doubted the cousin story, but she had no doubt about the underlying reason for Morris to be around. That leak had pushed everything into frenetic motion. There had been a huge public response. Morris would know about the latest lab results. He would know they had a three-month mooring window. And Morris being Morris, he wanted to capitalize now. There was an urgency in every conversation that Catherine herself struggled to feel. The *Red Pill 2.0* was close, Catherine would allow, but they could not do the full feature testing yet, meaning they were far short of releasing it to beta.

"Why not?" Morris asked.

"Because it's doesn't work the way it should," Catherine answered. "It's not perfect."

"Since when did you care about that? *Minimum viable product.* Ship something. Sell something. Since when do you hesitate? Since when do you second-guess?"

Tempers flaring in every meeting. Nothing like your vencap partner walking up and down between the desks and computers that he financed to make every other person in the place assume there's a bull's eye on your forehead. All the while that hit-counter on the wall that recorded the pre-registrations did not stop reminding them of what they were doing either. The import of it. The profile. The number of eyeballs on them. Fifteen million pre-registrations. Twenty million. Twenty-five, thirty. That was the number of interested parties. That was also the number of people watching and waiting.

"Do you know what happens at around fifty million firm pre-regs?" Morris asked her, sitting in the chair next to her workstation, kicking his feet up on a second chair he'd pulled over.

"I give up, Morris," Catherine said. "What happens?"

Well, what happened, Morris explained, was that the generated traffic started to matter much more than whatever it was that was generating the traffic.

"It becomes *about* the traffic," Morris said, with a smug smile.

"I am so not about the traffic," Catherine said in response. But here came that sinking hollow in her stomach again now. She could forget it, but then it did always return, with a phrase or a glance or a detail askew. Something hovering in the shadows, a shape at the farthest outlying point of peripheral vision, a glimmer there, a force awake in the world, not quite behind her, to one side, standing off at some distance and appraising critically, waiting for her next move as if to counter it. As if to bet against her in some key and incisive way. It made her cautious, that sense of invisible opposition. She saw that quite clearly. She was avoiding making the bet that the universe clearly needed her to lose.

Around her the Warehouse was buzzing. All that she had built and nurtured, agonized over. All somehow now critically at risk.

"The full feature test," Morris said, and his tone with her was quite gentle. "I need a firm date, Catherine."

She declined. They were getting there. Month end possibly. But no promises.

"Well then I think we need to talk," Morris said. And his words dropped onto the table between them. Catherine thought she felt a breeze, not cool or refreshing, a blast of something drying and very hot.

"Aren't we talking now?"

Something a little more formal. Something in Chicago. And Morris thought it might be a good time for her to figure out flying again, because they needed to do this soon. Next week.

"We don't have time for Amtrak," Morris said. "I'll let the partners know Thursday. Good?"

Catherine was slumped in her chair. *Partners.* Morris knocked on the desk with his knuckles, perhaps for luck. Then he left. And when Kali brought her noodles later, she didn't touch them. She hardly moved. She sat and thought of Rostock and all that he might mean. *Something that had happened to each of them. Something she needed to know.*

"Kali?" she called out across the Warehouse space, dust motes dancing in the last slanting rays of a setting sun.

Catherine was at her desk, drawer open. Fingers tight around a vial of pills. Ativan, Lorazepam. There were occasions now when she did not even consult the labels. "Kali," she called out.

And he was suddenly there. "Here," he said, voice almost a whisper. "Give me that. Let me help."

Perhaps no man had ever done something like that to her before, taken such direct control. Perhaps no man had ever dared. He took the pills from her hand. He returned them to the drawer.

"Madness," she whispered now, head in her hands.

Ximena sat poised with Kleenex she seemed to know would not be required as Catherine remembered the near-disaster of that evening. Kalmar and her, the last ones in the Warehouse. Kali and her chatting at the door. There were things that naturally followed one after another in situations like theirs, things human and chemical and necessary. You didn't talk about it. So Kali and Catherine, over dinner in Yaletown where he lived, didn't talk about it either. Just work and family, the food. Crispy calamari studded with toasted black garlic and chilies. A pork loin with miso broth and Hiroshimana greens. There were clicking chopsticks and conversations all around them in the dark room. The light fixtures were orbs, like glowing planets, like a galaxy in which they floated and gently spun. The booths were narrow and private. The sake was acid-sweet, at once fresh and soothing. Kali, she thought, looked oddly different than she'd seen him prior. Less inscrutable, he seemed now open, knowable. A striking man in that silvery light. Leanly muscled with those blue eyes and his full lips, a brooding slouch to his shoulders. He wore a black suit, white shirt with an open collar, evidence of a chain there. A Celtic cross, Catherine decided. Anchor tattoo on the back of one hand, dark beard, somewhat sparse, and flecked with grey despite him being short of thirty. And to notice these details also reminded her that she had not been out with a man, had not had sex since long-ago Liam, who'd dropped out of her life after a few days of bodyboarding in Cabo, never to be heard from again. She might have survived it, but AF801 still seemed on occasion to have swallowed her whole.

After dinner, they walked down to the water, where the wind set the rigging of moored sailboats into minute motion, wind chimes in the salty air. And then they were at the front door of his apartment, shining glass, water in the streets. Kalmar there at her shoulder. A light rain was turning the headlights of passing cars into an atmospheric blur. Catherine remembered distinctly catching her own reflection in the window of a passing taxi, a flash glimpse of her face on Kalmar's shoulder. He was hugging her gently. He was holding her, his hands on her hips. His lips were touching her ear. She realized how much she wanted this to happen, how much she wanted to be back at Kalmar's place, to see it, be inside it. All the while knowing with equal intensity that it could not happen, how terrible a decision it would be for her. Kalmar leading her through those doors, to the elevator, to that bed in the loft three floors above. Black sheets. Oblivion.

Impossible. The CEO and the markets director. Kalmar was the guy handling customers. For the lack of anybody else, he was also handling human resources. Morris would have a field day if he found out. He would need no more excuses. So it was thinking of Morris that she pulled away, just as Kalmar was reaching for her again, to draw her close. And out of an amused disgust with herself, with the trap of her own situation, she laughed, as if to dismiss this foolish thing that of course neither of them could actually have been considering seriously.

She thought the laugh had been a mistake. It was false anyway. But Catherine was known for her moments of sudden certainty, the tendency to cut options mercilessly, to winnow quickly to right answers. That's how Kalmar saw her in that moment. And he was angry with her. No words. But she saw it flash into his eyes, a hardening there, then a glance away into the traffic that flowed steadily past them, his shoulders hunched, chrome and neon glistening in the rising rain.

Ximena had listened for a long while at this point. No scribbled notes. No inserted questions. She waited now for several minutes as Catherine sipped her cold coffee and remembered these events.

"All the men," she said, finally.

Catherine seemed to awaken. She sat up straighter.

"Earlier," Ximena again, quietly insistent, "you said that all the men in your life seemed to have their separate demands."

Catherine nodded.

"Morris wants his big meeting," Ximena said.

Catherine with her face in her hands.

"And Kalmar . . . is in love?"

"Don't say that," Catherine said, through her fingers.

"Okay," Ximena agreed. "But he wants you in his bed I think, yes? Phil too, maybe?"

"No," Catherine said, lifting her head. "Phil is very sane that way."

Ximena nodded, unsmiling. "Okay, then. Who else?" Her head was cocked to one side, her gaze steady on the patient. And maybe Catherine should have come clean and acknowledged the last man in this tableau, the one who might in the end be the most demanding of all, the resurrection in her life of one of those sacred invisible few.

But Catherine knew at once that Ximena was not the person to whom that acknowledgement needed to be made. Here was not the place where Catherine clearly had to be heading, and heading as soon as possible.

That place, which Catherine saw with the clarity of an ecstatic vision, was Chicago.

TWO

I am alone and miserable; man will not
associate with me; but one as deformed and
horrible as myself would not deny herself
to me. My companion must be of the same
species and have the same defects. This being
you must create.

—MARY SHELLEY, *Frankenstein*

"YES, IN PERSON," CATHERINE WAS SAYING TO VALERIE. They were on the phone, as had long been their mid-week practice. Wednesday morning, midday. Valerie at home or in her shop. Catherine in her office, her chair swivelled around, looking out the window of the DIYagnosis Warehouse.

"And when?" her sister asked.

"Thursday next week."

"In Chicago. A guy phones asking you to meet him."

"Well that's where he lives, sister. And not just any guy. We do have this one thing in common."

"Right," Valerie said. "Chicago in mid-November. Take a warm coat."

"I will button up," Catherine said.

"Isn't this all maybe a bit creepy?"

"He didn't come off creepy at all," Catherine said. "He sounded pretty ordinary."

"This person who just calls. This doctor."

"He's an oncologist, retired. Used to work at the Comprehensive Cancer Center at the University of Chicago. He's legit. He checks out."

"Married?" Val said.

"Widowed. His wife died of breast cancer ten years ago."

"Oh. I'm sorry about that. Doctor who is it?"

Catherine told her again: Dr. Michael Rostock.

"Dinner in Chicago with Dr. Rostock," her sister said. "Thursday, as in a week tomorrow."

"And I'm flying there," Catherine told her.

"You're flying."

"I'm thinking of flying."

Catherine was looking at photos on the corner of her desk. Valerie, Mark. A nephew and a niece. Her entire family at that point.

"I'm thinking maybe this is the moment I choose to start flying again," Catherine said. "Chicago is what, four hours? It's not like France. And of course there will be drugs involved."

Val was at home that day, just now in the middle of negotiating some kitchen settlement between the kids. "Honey, you stop that, now. No. No. No."

She covered the phone with one hand. Then came back. "Sorry. I'm still thinking. Is this really a good idea for you right now?"

Catherine paused, hearing that familiar concern again in her sister's voice. Then she said, simply, "Dr. Rostock told me that he'd learned something about what happened to us."

Silence. "So what is it? What happened to you?"

"Well he didn't tell me on the phone, which is why we have to get together."

Dishes clattering. Something hitting the floor. Someone crying in the background. Catherine told Val she could call back but her sister said no. Then, "You don't really know this guy."

"I don't think he's dangerous. He's older. Quite dignified-looking, in fact."

"Dignified," Val said. "Well great. But that's not really what I'm talking about."

"We're meeting in a public place!" Catherine said. But she also knew that Valerie wasn't really talking about personal safety either. Her sister's concerns about her were by now highly generalized. Two years from a trauma like the one she'd endured was not a long time, in Valerie's opinion. Catherine should still be in therapy, Val thought. Catherine should be talking about things more openly. She should be letting herself breathe, not holding everything in and charging onwards. And here she was, heading off again in a whole new direction. Catherine could hear the caution in her sister's voice, even in her sister's silence.

"Don't worry about me," Catherine said.

Valerie sighed. "So why doesn't he fly to Vancouver if it's so urgent?"

He suggested that, Catherine explained. Only Catherine had to see Morris, so this worked just as well. "I mean, maybe this is also the moment," Catherine said. "I talk to Rostock and deal with the past. I sit down with Morris and sort out the future."

"That would be nice."

"That would be great!" Catherine said. Although she doubted she had grounds to hope for quite that much. She could picture Morris and his partners on the far side of that mahogany table, high views of the lakefront, Grant Park, the ice rink full of skaters. Michigan Avenue winking with Christmas lights.

"When Morris says *partners*," she had asked Phil, having called him late and at home. "Who would he be talking about exactly?"

Phil sounded sleepy. "Principals at his firm," he said. Parmer Ventures was a venture capital fund. As such, there would likely be people other than Morris with money in the pot. Morris played lead and managed the deals. But if anything went sideways, well, then they'd go to the group.

"Sideways?" Catherine said.

"Don't assume anything," Phil said, yawning. "Happens all the time. You have a product delayed in the pipeline to testing, which is holding up the beta release. So you're going to have people on the vencap side with questions. You just go down and tell them what's what."

Catherine remained dubious. And Phil seemed to sense it, adding a final note before they hung up. "Morris needs you more than you need him. And Morris is smart enough to know that," he said. "And yes, no worries. I'll be there."

Maybe Phil was right. Catherine tracked Morris down first thing the next morning. He was at an indoor driving range way up in Evanston on the north side of the city, he told her. She could hear the whack and whine of balls, imagined them heading out over the apple-green, AstroTurf fairway.

"About this meeting," she started. "This isn't you trying to fire me or something."

"Catherine, Catherine," Morris said, voice amused but not unkind. "I might be doing you a favour if I did."

"How d'you figure?"

"You with all your stresses and strains. You need a furlough. But I know your type."

"Do you? You sure?"

"I am sure," he said. "You are exactly like me as a younger man. And don't even pretend that offends you. When I first moved to this country I had your hunger, your drive. Never taking a break. Never taking my eye off the prize. I've since learned to take a breath once in a while."

"He was trying to give you advice," Valerie told Catherine, when she described the conversation. "I think he may have a point. Why don't you come with me to Provence next year?"

Maybe, she said. Maybe. And with that she let the conversation begin to drift through its regular closing waypoints. How things were going. How she was doing. Catherine told her sister the basic truth here, only slightly cleansed. She was going through a patch, a stretch. And she even found herself in partway, cautious agreement with Valerie that maybe, just maybe, looked at a certain way, Morris had a point about her taking time off. Maybe she should go to France and prowl the *brocante* markets for distressed chairs and teacups and unusual glass orbs. There was something to be said for simple, beautiful objects and the eye necessary to find them. And how terrible would it be in the end if Morris actually *did* offer to take out her position in DIY? Catherine was passionate about health. Surely this was a moment when she needed to be passionate about her own.

"You realize people dream all their lives about having even a minute to stop and think, recharge the batteries, right? You don't have to hang out with me. Go lie on the beach for a while. Any beach in the world."

Val had to go. More crying in the background. Plus she had to get down to the store later and meet an artisanal stained glass artist who was redoing her front window.

"Sounds expensive. You doing good otherwise?" Catherine said, realizing she hadn't asked about her sister at all.

"I'm doing amazing. We're stocking Christmas stuff now at the boutique. You should come over. Vintage mercury glass tree ornaments. Really nice."

Catherine couldn't remember the last time she'd even put up Christmas decorations. But she was sure that the objects in question would be beautiful.

"I'll try in the next couple weeks," she said. "Promise."

"I understand," her sister said. "You've got so much going on."

"Oh, I don't know. Anyway. Love."

"Love."

"Later."

"Bye-ee."

"Bye, Val."

She took the train. In the end, that's what it had to be. She'd thought she'd fly. Right to the last minute, she'd firmly believed it. She opened up the discount ticket site. She entered airports of departure and arrival. She pulled down the calendar and clicked on suitable dates.

Round trip. One adult. Preferred seat in the exit row, yes please. No checked luggage. No firearms, wheelchairs or surfboards.

No, I have not visited a farm in the past 30 days.

All done exactly as any ordinary person would until the moment her payment details had been entered—credit card number, expiry date, CVV code—and there was her cursor finally blinking over the confirmation button, and Catherine knew in a dizzying instant, even as her finger clicked the mouse and the purchase was completed, her credit card was billed, her heart pounding now, forehead beaded with sweat, chest empty, that she would never use the ticket. Even as the email confirmation arrived, she knew that she'd never been able, that she'd only been reviewing what it might have felt like to be normal in those moments, to do things routinely that now filled her with dread and panic, the sense of movement in her peripheral vision, the sense of threat, closeness. Black shapes, close and cold.

Amtrak is fine, she said to herself. Amtrak is great, really. And on the train she realized it really was, sitting in the suite she'd reserved. It was tiny, designed for two people to sit face to face. With just herself, she pulled the door shut, put her legs up on the opposite seat, wrapped a blanket around her and it was as if she were in a cozy nest. Very nice indeed. The landscape blurring past. Night falling. Two sleeps to Chicago. And after dinner and a glass of wine and turn-down service, she slept deeply and completely. Then woke and phoned Morris, having picked up a coffee and a Danish in the dining car. And she cut right to the chase.

"I'm looking forward to meeting your partners," she told him. The train was shuffling its way through eastern Montana by then, the flatlands spreading, bison on the ridge line. "I'm looking forward to answering any questions they may have."

"Well, that's super, Catherine," he said, letting out a breath. Not quite a sigh. There was a trace of irritability there. She was on the train, she'd just told him. She was going to be in a day late.

"May I know their names?" Catherine asked.

Morris didn't hide his exasperation. "Why are you even asking this? It's irrelevant."

"It's highly relevant," Catherine said. "I started this company, and if I'm going to let people sniff around in my business, I think I deserve to know their names."

"*We* started this company, Catherine. And you know my name." Then, gentler, "Where are you?"

"Just crossed the Continental Divide," she said.

Another pause. "You'll be flying again, soon enough," he said. He wasn't a bad man, despite his endless calculations and manoeuvres. "Come to town. We'll have a conversation and sort out the future. I'll let Kate and the others know you're a day behind."

Catherine heard her own name, the nickname her sister used. Phil too. Sometimes Yohai. But not Morris. "Confused here," she said. "You're talking to me now, yes?"

"Oh, sorry. Kate Speir," Morris said. "She's an advisor. Someone you might like to meet, actually. Tough as nails like you."

Catherine was staring out the glass as they spoke. She was thinking about what kind of person could advise Morris, who always seemed to have such developed plans of his own, his mind endlessly running the numbers in a hurry for the payoff. It must surely be someone tougher than Catherine herself felt at that moment, tucked under a blanket in a hurtling train, racing eastward towards a collision with God knows what. She could imagine that shotgun quite clearly now, the glinting length of it, barrels aimed directly at her.

Rostock came to mind just then and her mood steadied. She thought of the conversation they would have, the information and ideas and relevant experiences that such a man would carry. She wondered if Rostock would finally, on the approach of the two-year anniversary, stop the spread of shadows, throw light onto the mysteries.

And with that she let her forehead drift to the cool glass, to feel the rails thrumming there, to feel the landscape rolling past underneath her. The trained rocked and creaked. She was asleep in minutes. And it seemed like a mere blink before she woke to find herself pounding into Chicago, towers rising all around her. In a taxi, a hotel room, a long bath, all in what seemed like a kaleidoscopic minute, a tumbling of colour and movement and mood. Dinner, then sleep. And then it was the morning of the day in question, and she was fresh and ready. And up that elevator she went in that gleaming black tower on Randolph Avenue, up into the clouds, to the boardroom with its globe and telescope, with its shining expanses of mahogany. And Morris. No flanking lawyers, accountants, no advisors. Just Morris stern-faced on the far side of the table, hands folded in front him. Black crewneck, Apple watch. Check, check. Black teleconference console at his elbow, one red light blinking to signal another presence there.

Phil too. Phil who pushed his big frame up out of the black leather swivel chair on the near side of the table opposite Morris, took her hand in both of his, bending down to greet her with a kiss to her cheek.

Catherine scanned the room for effect, noting the men in turn, the emptiness around the rest of the table, that single blinking light. But Morris didn't wait for her to comment. He began immediately once she'd sunk into her chair. No deck of PowerPoint slides. Everything he had to say was prepared and waiting merely for the cue to be released. And here it came. A single finger to a button on the teleconference console. A blinking red light gone solid green. And then all the anomalous details of this performance were swamped immediately and forgotten in the jolting explosion, the shuddering shock waves carried towards her by what Morris went on to say.

"Catherine," he began, voice hard and flat. "We'd like you to listen to a couple of key points. We think they're really important. And we think that you will soon agree."

CLIENT CONFLICT

MORRIS WAS FORCING HER OUT. Or that's what it worked out to after you did the math. Morris was giving her thirty days' notice of his intent to activate the buy-sell agreement, to pull the trigger on that shotgun. Thirty days after which Catherine either gave up her company or raised the same amount he'd offered and bought him out.

All Catherine could feel in the numb twenty-five minutes of that meeting was that she'd made that whole trip across the continent only to find out that Morris didn't have any surprises for her. He was exactly the man she'd seen all along. He was even dressed the same as the last time she'd been in that room. The perfect uniform for the man who would drag her here for this ritual humiliation and not just do her the courtesy of writing an email and letting her flush deep red in private.

Morris sat impassively at the head of that dark wood table as he spoke, the sea of navy carpet around them. All those clubby details she remembered, the cowboy art and the cigar box on a sideboard. Catherine had taken the same seat by the window where she had received Morris's flattery the last time round. Grant Park, Butler Field, the lake beyond. It was a brilliantly sunny day and the towers along Randolph and Michigan were gleaming.

When Phil had leaned close to kiss her cheek on her arrival earlier, he'd whispered: "Hear him out. Then we respond."

So she listened while Morris spoke, his hands folded in front of him, only unfolding at certain moments when he would raise a finger to tap it on the dark wood surface to emphasize a point. Morris had a new investment partner, he explained. A private fund called Mako Equity. They'd taken an interest in DIY and wanted to be involved. But Mako, Morris said, played alone. And they were too many years in and too many billions returned to change practice now. That meant they were asking him for a new CEO. And the best way to accommodate that demand was to give Catherine this opportunity to sell.

"Opportunity?" Catherine said, incredulous, receiving a fractional side-glance from Phil who had, as always, adopted the practice of listening fully before responding in any way.

It was a big number, Morris said. DYI market valuations had soared. "No sane person turns this down."

"Sane. Sorry, what are you saying?" Catherine shot back.

"Let's hear the details and then consider whether responding now or in a few days might be better," Phil said to her.

Morris had produced a letter from an inside pocket that he laid on the table next to him, edges neatly aligned with the corner of the table. The theatrics were obvious. As if the money were actually in the envelope right there and she had to snatch it before Morris changed his mind. Catherine felt a bitter laugh rising, but suppressed it feeling sure she'd sound hysterical.

"What about the courtesy of a conversation?" Catherine said. "What about we try to sort things out between us?"

She'd meant that as a bid for reason. But the words came out sounded pleading and weak. Why would she even suggest that? Morris had insulted her by being this predictable. No sane person would want to work with him after that.

"We've had many conversations," Morris said, sitting back. "And things have still not progressed as I believe they should."

But there was no judgment here, Morris went on. It was no shame to have been distracted after what she'd been through. It was normal, and it was the way the mind and the body returned to health.

"Morris?" Catherine said. "Drop it. I'm completely healthy and don't appreciate the insinuation."

"We're not here to talk about your performance. We're executing the buy-sell because that's what our partnership agreement allows either of us to do at any time."

"You're not executing," Phil interjected. "You're notifying your intent as stipulated in the agreement. I'd also like to point out that having notified, it's entirely possible to withdraw the notification in the thirty-day period if both parties agree."

"Well, I wouldn't hold your breath," Morris said. "Mako are very keen. They won't walk away. Catherine, you really need to think seriously about this. It's a lot of money."

"An amount I could raise privately and buy your share."

Morris raised his eyebrows and shoulders together slightly. *Sure. Of course. You could.*

She turned to Phil.

"Technically, yes," he said. "But probably best to discuss that possibility in private."

But what Phil wasn't saying was obvious to all. There was a certain art to the triggering of a buy-sell, the choosing of a price that you knew your partner could never match. Morris had far more resources at his disposal now than Catherine ever would herself. With Mako Equity in the picture, she didn't stand a chance.

"There is one other thing that I might mention," Morris said, and here he looked away from her, and she sensed something slightly different incoming. Here came the threat. "Mooring," he said.

This was not what Catherine had been expecting.

"You didn't tell me that you'd gotten it stable at three months. I had to learn that from Dr. Burke."

Phil once again gave her a half glance, curious. But she didn't say anything. Now wasn't the time to explain. And of course Morris was right. She hadn't told him. She'd suppressed that information because she knew he'd force the prototype into test. The atmosphere around testing and launching was clouded, Catherine thought. They needed to have everything lined up. Everything sorted.

Morris was talking again, slowly and steadily. And here came the threat she'd sensed earlier. After activating the buy-sell, if Mako came to the conclusion that she was acting in bad faith, they would sue.

Phil took a breath, let it out. "Do we have to go here right now?" he asked.

"No, we don't," Catherine said. "But let's. Bad faith how?"

"Well," Morris said, "if decisions you make with your time remaining are seen to erode DIY market position . . ."

"Give me a break," Catherine said. "Everything I've done has been to advance our interests."

"I'm not saying differently. But it's a matter of a third party's perception. Speaking personally, I'm drawn more to a different analysis."

Catherine waited.

"Seems to me," Morris said, with muted but still evident satisfaction, "that your delays brought about this offer. You attracted this attention to yourself."

"I'm not sure this is productive," Phil said.

"Might as well go ahead, Morris," Catherine said.

Well, he explained, Mako was obviously attracted to the DIY valuation. But they wouldn't invest if they didn't think that valuation was going to go higher. "If you had pushed the product through testing to beta release as I advised," Morris said, "our valuation would now be so high that Mako wouldn't touch it."

"I'm quite sure this isn't productive," Phil said.

The discussion had shifted in tone so distinctly that Catherine felt it like the temperature rising in the room. She was still flushed red. Only now she thought she might be sweating along her brow.

This suggestion that it was *she* who had authored this situation. And that idea of having brought this threat onto herself suddenly refocused Catherine not on Morris but on that teleconference console in the middle of the table, on that solid green light. Someone was listening there. Someone who had said not a word, whom Catherine had not even heard shuffling papers or breathing. Somewhere out there, an invisible other was listening to her and listening carefully. Catherine's chest was full to bursting, and she came forward out of her chair, hands to the table, to her feet now. Phil went to stand up himself. She saw his weight go sharply forward in his chair, the leather squelching. But then when she only leaned forward and snatched the envelope from in front of Morris—who didn't resist it, who seemed to have anticipated exactly that motion—Phil sat back. He did not reach out a hand towards her, to restrain her as he might have thought necessary, to calm her or to intervene in any other way.

Catherine stood punching the button for the elevator even though it was already summoned and on its way, humming up the shaft to rescue her, take her clean away. She didn't say a word until the car had arrived, the doors ghosting open. Phil's hand across the light beam as she stepped inside. Then the doors breathed shut and they were plummeting earthwards. She gripped the rail. She remembered as always the sensation of tipping, falling. She closed her eyes, briefly nauseous, but forced them open.

"Well that went just about as badly as possible, didn't it?"

Phil was staring up at the monitor in the top corner of the car: a stock ticker, a talking head. He was hard to read at the best of times, and was now merely looking lost in thought.

"Mako Equity?" Catherine said. "Did I actually get that right? Morris is partnered with a company named after a predator fish? What do these people think, this is a freaking movie?"

"They definitely do not think that," Phil said. "We should talk. Time for a drink?"

"Dinner plans, actually," Catherine said. "But yes, a quick one. We definitely need to talk."

The car was braking. Catherine could feel the incremental Gs, the sense of mounting weight and then a springing back, a new lightness.

Phil led her to a place around the corner. They entered a long white marble room with black stools and hundreds of bright bottles behind the counter. By the time they were seated and had ordered, Catherine was back to fuming.

"So that's where we're at," Catherine said. "Anybody can sue anybody. Anybody can make accusations about my mental state."

"Nobody said anything about your mental state," Phil said.

"You heard him going on about my *distractions*. That's code for hysteria, Phil. That's what men say to women in these sorts of meetings. And these guys in tech can be the worst dickheads of all. And why didn't the Mako people say anything? What is up with that? They're on the phone but not a word? Silence. Nada. Zip. Doesn't that strike you as hostile?"

"It strikes me as careful," Phil said, just as the drinks arrived. A beer for him and glass of pinot noir for her. He took a sip, looking into the bar mirror. "So what's on for dinner? If I may ask."

Catherine took a breath. It had been several hours since she'd thought of Dr. Rostock and whatever it was that he so urgently had to tell her. She realized, sitting there with Phil, that she had a number of questions she wanted to ask the good doctor also. Someone who'd been there and felt what she had felt.

"Oh, don't answer," Phil said, with a small and wistful smile. "Not prying. Just asking."

"An old friend," Catherine said. "Now let's talk about what we're actually going to do here, *consigliere*."

Phil reacted to the nickname, sipping again, then setting the drink down with a small sigh signalling that whatever he felt it was necessary to say just then, as *consigliere*, he'd rather he didn't.

"Talk to me."

"All right," he said. "To be clear, though, before we begin: nothing that I'm about to tell you was known to me before 8:00 p.m. yesterday evening. I learned all this after our last conversation."

"And what have you learned?"

"Well, as we know, the possibility of legal action is real."

"Right," Catherine said, sipping her wine. "I've been thinking about that. I mean, just these past few minutes. What about if we sue Morris first?"

Phil sat back a bit, surprised. But his expression already told her what he thought of that idea. "Cate, listen . . ."

"No, no. Just hear me out. You said it yourself: anybody can sue anybody. So we go after him pre-emptively."

"On what grounds?" Phil asked.

"The partnership agreement with that buy-sell was drafted by his lawyers."

"You had independent advice before signing it."

"Not from you. You were on Saturna Island and I spoke to one of your partners."

Phil sighed. "So you sue Morris. You sue one of my partners for giving you bad advice . . ."

"I'm not handing Morris this company, especially not after the insult of that meeting."

"Cate, with respect and real affection, I think you should listen to yourself. Morris is offering you far more money than you ever would have thought possible when you started out."

"How do you know? Maybe I was imagining lots of money."

"I don't think you were," Phil said. "You live modestly. Small apartment. You use a car share. You're not a money-driven person. You're letting this issue get mixed up with a lot of other things."

"Oh, I see," Catherine said.

Phil took a sip of his beer. "Let me play back to you what I'm hearing. Okay? It's a cash offer, in effect. But you don't want it. You want to have a big fight instead and pay a lot of big legal bills in a dispute I don't think you'd win and the net result of which certainly wouldn't be a better state of mind for you."

Catherine closed her eyes for a second. Of course he was making sense. Phil always made sense. But then Morris came back to her, his avuncular, shoulder-patting condescension, sitting like Buddha behind that desk while some strange other listened carefully from the far end of a silent phone line. Who was that? Who was that person who had taken a sudden shine to the things that Catherine herself had so deeply cared about?

"Phil," she said, opening her eyes. "We could make it a good case. Shotgun clauses favour the partner with deep pockets. Everybody knows that. We argue that it was well known Morris had certain resources and I was a cashless entrepreneur whose patents needed millions in development funding to even test whether they could be commercial. I was financing myself on savings and credit cards, Phil. Anyone advising me to sign that agreement would have been negligent, their legal advice void and my signature invalid. No partnership agreement, no buy-sell, no exit provision, and Morris can take his offer and stuff it exactly where I should have told him to."

"You could make that argument, of course," Phil said. "You could make a lot of arguments. It doesn't mean you'd win."

"But we wouldn't have to win," Catherine said, leaning forward and grabbing Phil's arm. "Mako doesn't want any part of a lawsuit. We sue and his partners run, Phil. And without them Morris's offer vaporizes."

"You don't know that," Phil said. "But my bigger point—"

"You write them a good letter, Phil. I can pay you for that much."

"I know you can," Phil said. "But this is where we get to the heart of the matter, Cate. I can't do what you're asking me to do."

"What are you talking about? You're my lawyer. You're a partner in one of the biggest, scariest law firms in the country. Your litigators are animals."

"Maybe they are, Cate. But *I* can't do this for *you*."

Catherine had been looking past him down the bar while he spoke, but this one brought her back sharply. "Why not?" she said.

He sat back on his stool, rocking slightly in place. People were streaming into the bar, the volume rising. Someone brushed by Phil so closely that he had to lean sharply to one side and they were briefly pressed shoulder to shoulder. She could smell him. No cologne. Just an attractive cottony clean.

"Why not for me, Phil?" she said again, when he'd returned to his original position.

Phil sighed. "Because, in the event of a lawsuit—launched either by you or them—the firm would be in client conflict."

"Client conflict how?"

"We'd be on both sides."

"You're telling me you represent Morris separately?"

"Not Morris," Phil said. "Mako. And not me, obviously. But another partner. This has just come to my attention. I can't say more for reasons of confidentiality. But it's a fact. My firm represents Mako Equity in separate matters."

Catherine sat back. "Oh, Phil."

Phil sat looking into his beer, one hand around the base of the glass, turning it, turning.

"How long have you represented them?" she asked.

He shook his head. He couldn't say.

"Wasn't I your client first?"

"This is the part where I need you to understand I didn't know until yesterday," Phil said, voice low and measured. "When a conflict like this is identified, the firm has to make a decision about which client will be retained and which will be asked to seek other representation. The partners' Client Conflict Group made that call yesterday. I do not sit on that committee. They called and informed me. I'm really sorry."

"You're firing me," Catherine said. She was flushing, her leg was trembling.

"I'm not," he said, voice now urgent. "If there's no lawsuit then there's no conflict."

"You mean if I sign . . . Oh my God, and you don't see what's going on here, do you? Mako is playing you. They want this deal for a reason, Phil. Because they're stealing this company from me. And to make sure I can't even fight a proper legal fight, they steal my counsel at the same time. When did Mako's business walk in the door, Phil? How many days ago? How many days before Morris tabled his offer? Don't answer. I know."

Catherine felt sick, like she'd been punched in the stomach. Oxygen deficiency and a spreading numbness within.

Phil took a big breath. Then he leaned forward and brought his face quite close to hers. Voice almost a whisper now.

"I would never knowingly deceive you," he said. "I think you know me well enough to believe that. And I'm going to go one step further. I think you also know that the time has come to walk away. I know you can do it. You're the kind of person who can. I knew you before the accident, Cate. And I've seen you struggle since. Maybe Morris turns DIY into his billion-dollar unicorn, rides the whole thing to some huge exit. But honestly? Probably he doesn't. Probably he screws it up. Probably some kids in Delhi are working on exactly the same idea. Probably a hundred things. In the meantime his offer is a good one and would allow you to step back and think about yourself for a while. Yourself. Your health. Your future."

Phil the eminently reasonable. Phil who actually cared about her as a person. Phil who, it wasn't hard to see, under different circumstances for both of them might well have been something more.

Catherine was nodding to herself now. But for all his understanding, Phil still wasn't getting it. He wasn't getting what it felt like to have someone swivel their attentions on you, decide that what you had built, what you had cared for, what you had now within your grasp might very conceivably be their own.

"So I sign," Catherine said. "Your best advice."

Phil was listening carefully, poised on his stool, as if a sudden move might ruin a delicate balance.

"I sign and then what happens?" she asked him.

"Whatever you want to have happen, Cate. Take a holiday. Start something new. There are many more potential success stories in your life."

"No, I mean with respect to the in-firm conflict you're telling me about here. What happens with that?"

"Well, if you sign the sale agreement," Phil said, "there will be no lawsuit and therefore no conflict."

"So that's where we are."

"Cate, please sit down."

But something had stormed back into her and now would not let her go. She was up already, pulling on her coat. "Only thing you're forgetting, Phil, is that if I sign and sell I won't be needing a lawyer any more, will I?"

She heard him get up as if to follow her, just as she turned away. And she heard him call her name, once and then again.

SHE SAT IN HER HOTEL ROOM, TRYING NOT TO MOVE. It was her form of meditation, more of a physical than a mental thing. She'd never been able to do the regular kind of meditation, emptying your brain of thoughts and all that. She liked a clean apartment and modern furniture, but the inside of her head, she once joked to Valerie, was more like a Hieronymus Bosch painting. So: still the body, hope for the best.

Her eyes blinked open now. She rolled off the bed to the phone.

"I was mad," she said, when he picked up. Phil was in a taxi on his way to O'Hare. "I'm still mad."

"I'm not happy with the situation myself," he said. "Will you be all right?"

"I'll be fine," she told him. "Two things. First, I need you to be Phil for a minute here, not a partner from that heartless mega-firm that just refused to represent me."

"I can do that," he said.

"Second, I need a referral."

"I see," Phil said. "So, full speed ahead and sue the world."

"Maybe. But if I do that I'll be needing a lawyer and it seems I've misplaced mine."

"I'll find you someone," Phil said. "Although my opinion about it remains the same."

"I appreciate your opinion. You know that. I'm a big girl, though. All grown up."

"I'm being quite serious here," Phil said. "You should be careful."

And now something in his tone had changed. There was a trace of emotion there.

"Don't be so sure Mako Equity runs away if you sue. And if you actually got the fight you would be asking for, you might regret the outcome. Morris Parmer is Morris Parmer. You know him pretty well. Mako, you don't know."

"What are you trying to tell me?" Catherine asked. "What should I know?"

"I can't really answer that," Phil said.

"They're scary somehow," she said.

"I don't know very much," he said. Then there was a pause. "Mako is a black hole. I've only spoken briefly to my partners who deal with them. But even they don't know much."

"Isn't that all rather odd?"

"Yes," Phil said. "It is a bit."

"Who is Kate Speir?" she asked. She had intended to keep this information to herself, thinking that it might be of significance at some future point in time. But maybe this was that future moment she'd been imagining.

Phil's long pause suggested she was on to something. Finally he came back with a slow question, "Who gave you that name?"

"Morris," she said. "He said she was an *advisor*."

"I'm surprised," Phil said. "What else did he say?"

"Nothing."

"I'm way out on a limb here," Phil said.

"Tell me."

"As best I can make out, Speir is Mako's managing partner. Either that or she *is* Mako," Phil said. "It's a private equity fund, but she's the only name I've heard in connection with it."

"Private equity."

"Morris Parmer's bank, essentially."

"What do they want with DIY?"

Phil didn't have a clue and he didn't want to speculate either.

"So they fund Morris. He buys me out."

"That's the idea."

"And then what role do you see them playing?" Catherine said.

"Being private equity, they'll buy to control. And if they control they'll almost certainly install their own leadership."

"Speir herself."

"I doubt it. These funds generally bring in talent or promote internally."

"Well, well," Catherine said, imagining Hapok or Yohai or Kalmar in charge of the show. But more pointedly imagining this force that really opposed her now, consolidated and solidified into the shape of a single person. "And where is this mystery fund based?" she said.

"I heard Seattle," Phil said. "Does it matter?"

The news unsettled her more than she might have anticipated. Because it was close? An hour by air from Vancouver? Phil was right that it didn't matter. But the whole business had an increasingly *off* aroma about it. The whole Kate and Cate thing, though Catherine also knew just how loony it would sound for her to admit even thinking that to Phil, or anyone. Money was impersonal, objective. It didn't care about names or places.

"I take it the fund is big," she said.

"It's big," Phil said. "Call it billions and don't torment yourself."

"Billions," Catherine said. "Dealing arms or meth?"

"Pretty sure neither. But going further I'd be guessing," Phil said. "And now I have to stop being friend Phil, which I really do enjoy with you, and go back to being lawyer Phil. Okay? So I'm not going to say anything more."

Catherine didn't object. It was time to go. So they said goodbye nicely and promised to speak again on her return to Vancouver. And after hanging up, she got up and stood in front of the floor-length mirror appraising herself in its reflection, hands on her hips. She stroked her hair back behind both ears, looked carefully at her face. The cheekbones, the symmetry of jawline and chin.

That was Catherine Bach there, looking back at her. Founder and CEO of DIYagnosis Personal Health Systems. And she remembered then what had existed with such clarity before AF801, her bid to bring something real and powerful and rational to people everywhere, a degree of control over the mysteries within. Data, information, knowledge, autonomy. That was the Stephen Hawking country in which she had always preferred to roam. Freedom based on rational inquiry. And maybe some of that sense of freedom had crashed with her on that terrible day, spent along with the last units of her life's luck such that she might even have seen a glimmer of the upside in simply letting DIY go, taking some time on a beach just as Valerie had said.

But no more. She would not fall from the sky to a pebbly beach, then go sleep away her life on a sandy one. And she would definitely not let someone, some shadow form, silent in the phone lines, take from her what she had herself built out of blood and determination.

AF801, 2L. Tonight she was going to rise from that fated seat, take back some control, and head on through the business class cabin to 70F, to find who was fated at those coordinates too. A certain Dr. Michael Rostock, whom she visualized sitting quietly, legs crossed, reading a book on his iPad there.

Rostock had suggested a restaurant in the Fulton River District called The Ravenswood. And the moment she climbed out of the taxi, it seemed to her that this was exactly the place where their meeting should occur. The old warehouses now lofted and gentrified. The coffee shops and genteel bars, the organic produce stands and dog washing salons. Of course they had to be in a part of

Chicago that was reinventing itself. They had themselves fallen from the sky, both of them still figuring out what they had become.

The Ravenswood itself was in a low-slung structure with angular glass and external sheets of corrugated aluminum. Inside, a narrow room stretching away in chambers farther back, with blue-tinged lighting and crisp modern furniture.

She spotted Rostock the moment she pushed open the heavy, glazed-glass front doors. She knew him from the picture, yes. But also because he stood right away, evidently having been watching the door. He had a kind face, but with a regal accent to it. And when she crossed the room to greet him, he took her hand in both of his and shook with a slight inclination of his head. A man of manners, with one foot in an older and more cordial time.

"How did your meeting go?" he asked, when they were seated.

"Let's see," Catherine said to him, as the waiter pulled up to her elbow, "how's this for an answer: I'll have a gin Gibson, please. Rocks."

Rostock ordered prosecco. And when the waiter was gone, he said, "We don't have to talk about it."

"I don't mind," she said. "I'm having a fight with my business partner."

He cocked his head, curious.

"It's complicated," she said. "Vencap money."

Rostock was listening, but she could see he wasn't understanding.

"Sorry," she said. "Venture capital."

"Right," he said. "These are the folks who provide money to you bright young people with ideas."

"Not always so bright or young," she said. "The short version is I brought him in too early, which is exactly what I said I would never do and then went ahead and did, probably because I was flattered by the attention, and then of course as these things go we started having slightly different visions of the future and he went and produced this big equity partner with deeper pockets than God,

which, combined with a partnership agreement with exit provisions I never should have signed, basically allows him to write a
cheque and force me out."

Rostock was listening intently.

"Sorry," she said. "I'm ranting."

He didn't seem to mind, only shook his head and made a sympa-
thetic expression. And when their drinks arrived, he raised his glass
towards her and said, "To better days."

"*Prosit*," she said, and sipped, enjoying the slurry burn of it, the
settling of it into her, the settling of herself into the chair. Then,
looking across the table at Rostock, she said, "I sort of don't know
what to say. Us sitting here."

He nodded slowly, setting his glass down delicately on the white
linen tablecloth. "Let me start then with thank you, again, for
coming. I can only imagine what you thought of me when I first
called. Very forward. Impolite even."

He had a tiny defect in his left eye, Catherine noticed. A sickle
trace of black across the lower iris, as if the eye had once been
injured there and scarred.

"I don't know about impolite," she said. "Maybe what you're
doing is healthy."

"You think so?"

"Well, since the accident I haven't talked much about it, even
though it's been impossible not to remember and think about.
Dreams. Nightmares, really. The first year wasn't so bad. This
second year, seems like things have been moving somehow. Things
going on. Things getting . . ." she stumbled here. *Things getting
what?* "Complicated."

"Yes," Rostock said. "I sense that and I'm not at all surprised."

"So you've been in touch with the others," Catherine said. "Tell
me about them. Tell me what you've learned."

But before Rostock could answer, the waiter sidled in to run through the specials. He was bearded and plump with floral tattoos on both wrists and tight red jeans. He told them about tempura soft shell crab and an elk loin poached in duck fat. Catherine registered only then that the place did smell great, delicately herbed and charred. She was hungry.

"To your question," he said, when the young man had left. "I haven't actually spoken with any of the others although I have been calling. But I haven't actually gotten through to anyone but you."

Catherine frowned. "I'm sorry. I misunderstood."

"Well, you couldn't have known this next part."

Catherine was nearly finished her drink already, which was mildly alarming. She said, "And what next part is that?"

"They're gone, Catherine." Rostock cleared his throat and looked distinctly uncomfortable. Then he gathered himself, tightening his own resolve. He looked across the table at her evenly, unblinking. "The other four survivors," he said. "They're all dead. And in each case, it was suicide."

Catherine's eyes went briefly wide. As the waiter passed nearby she held up her hand, and when he came over she ordered another Gibson.

"Since this isn't a date," she said to Rostock, "I'm not going to worry about you thinking I'm a lush."

"I understand," he said. "I've just shared strange and troubling news."

"Four suicides," she repeated.

Rostock nodded, expression grim. He had the facts. He'd done his research. He'd been working his way down the list, trying to make contact with the survivors one by one. "I had a seat plan," he said. "Economy, Business, First. I didn't know how else to tackle it."

So it was that when Catherine picked up the phone, Rostock knew those other stories. On the lower deck of the A380-800, 12B was Nancy Whittle. She was from Kent, England, took Ryan Air to Paris for a cheaper flight over to see relatives in Illinois. 18E was

Adrian Janic, thirty-three, a Serbian carpenter hoping to work under the table. 20F was a student named Patricia Langston returning home from three months of European travel. 63B was Douglas Marshall, just ahead of Rostock in the upper-deck business cabin, an insurance executive based in Paris.

Catherine, who had so deliberately avoided knowing the names prior, leaned forward into the table now. Nancy, Adrian, Patricia, Douglas. There was a quality to this kind of news. Catherine fished around for it a minute, wondering what experience she'd had before that seemed similar. Then she had it: news of family members. What Valerie had been doing after they'd been unable to speak for a while. News of the kids, even Mark. People bonded to you through no choice of your own, and in whose health you were somehow organically invested.

"Go on," she said to Rostock.

They had a range of injuries afterwards, Rostock had discovered. Pat Langston by far the worst, with what he learned was lower spinal cord damage that kept her in a wheelchair for the remaining months of her life. For the others he didn't have specifics.

"Medical records are confidential, obviously. And you don't want to ask families about these sorts of things. Even as a doctor . . ." Rostock's voice trailed off.

"But the families told you," Catherine said to him.

They did, eventually. "That's part of what really gripped me about this coincidence. In each case, when the families found out I was a doctor and that I'd been on that plane and survived, they wanted me to know that something had gone terribly wrong with these people they loved. After being lucky, after defying the odds, after all of that came something else. Lives going off the rails. Some terrible wrong turning."

"This is very disturbing," Catherine managed.

Rostock nodded. "In Nancy Whittle's case, the family, four

children, all healthy and with families of their own, didn't tell me it was a suicide at first. But as it happened, I called the eldest daughter after the others. So I knew what had happened to the other three. Honestly, I was making that phone call with a significant degree of dread. I wanted to stop. But I had to know. So I called, and when I learned she'd died—she said natural causes—I mentioned that at least three of the other survivors had since died as well. All in quite a narrow time frame. And that really struck her. I could hear it on the phone. She asked me: How? How did they die? Then I told her, and she broke down in tears and out came the story. Her mother had been severely depressed. She'd developed paranoid delusions. Thought she was being followed, that her phone was being tapped. She'd begun to isolate herself, cutting off family members."

"And the others?"

"Variations on a theme," Rostock said. Patricia Langston and Adrian Janic had apparently been hit by depression soon after release from the hospital. Depression, delusions, paranoia. They were both gone in a few months.

Catherine was struggling to process this information, staring at Rostock, shaking her head. "So by the time you got to me," she said finally, "you were wondering what you'd find."

"I knew you were alive from Google News," Rostock said. "And, I'll be honest, your story felt different. You seem to have a lot on the go. I'm not a psychiatrist, but distractions are probably a blessing in the face of these things."

Catherine was watching him closely. It occurred to her then that Rostock was, in a sense, right. What really filled her mind, outside those moments when she looked at that seat plan and recited the numbers, gazing over the lip of the day and into blackness? She thought about the second prototype. She thought about mooring tech and being behind schedule. She thought about timetables and flow charts and the reasons why she was holding back. She thought about Morris and Kalmar, Yohai, Hapok, and most recently she thought about Mako and Kate Speir, a distraction that Catherine imagined growing more significant with each passing hour. She was long on distractions, she thought, they were her central project.

Rostock was looking at the table. Catherine leaned forward. "I'm glad you told me. It's terrible news. I don't understand it. But I'm still here," she said. "Most important, I'm okay. Really, I am. I'm stressed but not depressed."

He nodded. "Well, good. Of course I wondered. But I'm relieved and encouraged to see you healthy and optimistic."

"I'm not sure about *optimistic*," she said. "But I'm alive and realistic with fight in me yet."

He smiled, finally. "All right," he said. "I'm glad to hear it. I really am."

A moment of silence fell between them. She refolded her napkin on her lap and he twirled his flute of prosecco. Then he sat forward sharply, hands folded precisely in front of him.

"63B, Douglas Marshall," Rostock said. "His story was especially interesting to me."

There was something beyond depression and paranoia in the insurance executive's case. Even his family seemed to sense it. Marshall had become extremely volatile and angry, even violent on occasion. He was gripped by fear.

"In the end, he cut his own throat with a box cutter."

Catherine's hand shot up involuntarily to cover her own throat. "Oh my God."

"They found him several days later. But here's the important thing. He seems to have left a suicide note."

Catherine waited for it, vague dread mounting.

"*I'm following myself. I will catch myself. And then we'll see who wins.*"

Catherine squinting, trying to make sense of it.

Rostock nodded grimly, poised to say something further. And

Catherine processed the hesitation, feeling the evening turn as if on a pivot.

"Go ahead," she said to Rostock. "This is leading somewhere. The thing you really wanted to tell me. It's something that happened to you."

Catherine sat quite still, waiting for it. She wasn't going anywhere. She was going to stay there and listen to Rostock's story, because she could not bear the thought of not knowing it.

The waiter was there, at her elbow. He provided the punctuation mark required by the moment. A breath, a quick scan of the menu, the music in the room ramping a degree in volume, the door to the kitchen swinging open and disgorging plates that dispersed throughout the room. The light seemed to green out slightly, deepening in texture and tone, as if the restaurant were an enormous glass submarine that had just slipped soundlessly beneath the waves, carrying them all downward.

THEY FUSSED WITH THE MENU, disappearing into that for several ritual moments. It had descriptions of the farms where ingredients were procured, pictures of smiling farmers over short bios and quotes. Catherine read one aloud.

"We're only truly secure when we can look out our kitchen window and see our food growing and our friends working nearby."

She looked up. Rostock was listening. Curious and amused.

"Like during the Irish potato famine," Catherine said. "Or the Dark Ages."

He laughed. It was good to hear.

Glasses of wine arrived. Rostock sipped and murmured, "Very nice." And when the bread came, he took a piece, holding it gingerly before placing it on a silver-rimmed side plate.

"I'm sixty-two," he began. "Sixty when it all happened. I had reason to be in Paris for a conference before Christmas. I hadn't been there since my last time with Angela, my wife. She loved Paris. We took other holidays, but that was the one place she really always wanted to return to. We stayed on Le Rue Serpente. Walked everywhere. Had our set of favourite cafés and restaurants."

That first trip back since Angela's death had been melancholy, Rostock admitted. He was busy during the day. But at night, his feet found their own rhythm. The feet remembered. And so they took him down the streets where they knew to walk, all the places he and Angela had been together. From the square outside Saint-Sulpice, up through the gardens and into the Avenue de l'Observatoire. Around the corner and down the Boulevard du Montparnasse. Le Select was of course open and bustling, one of the old favourites. It was cold out. And Rostock said he was tempted go in, sit down to the smoked salmon salad, the *côte de veau à la Normande*.

"What we called our *prom date dinner*," Rostock said with a smile, which then faded. "But that would have been too much."

Rostock ate some bread. He was in new territory talking about all this, Catherine could tell. Perhaps he had few close and trusted friends himself. Perhaps he was like her in that way too, surrounded largely by the complications of hostile colleagues and worried family.

After a few days, Rostock said, the conference wrapped. He'd presented a paper, gone to bed and woken early as planned. He remembered a gorgeous Parisian morning, rose light, the hum of early traffic in the streets and the café below his window.

"A real threshold moment," he said. "I was booked to fly out. But everything seemed to be perfectly arranged to convince me that I should extend my stay. Reclaim Paris, as it were. Angela would have loved for me to do that."

But he didn't. He woke that morning and smelled the coffee and fresh-cut narcissus in the vase on his bedside table. He thought of his wife and this only sped up his thoughts about home. He packed up quickly, hurrying. He rode the train to Charles de Gaulle and arrived feeling as though the right thing had been done. And on the plane, on that doomed flight, he sat with a smile of satisfaction on his face. He felt *unified*, he said, the most accurate way he could think to describe it. He felt wholly himself again.

Both of them were now thinking of themselves in their seats, waiting for takeoff. When that seatbelt light winked on, they weren't even that far apart. Poised together before all that would follow. The surge of the huge jet turbines, the flattening of their spines into their seats, the rake of the nose as it vaulted from the runway, then the steep climb. Up and up, then rolling north and westward, out over the U.K. towards the Irish Sea. Half past ten in the evening.

"Then what happened, happened," Rostock said.

"Yes," Catherine said. "It did."

His expression sharpened. His voice dropped. "And by the time we were in the afterwards, something had happened to me. I felt it in my blood and bones. That unity I'd felt was gone. I'd been split and scattered. As if I'd been separated into parts and was quite possibly missing some."

He was looking away from Catherine now, out through the front window and into the flowing, darkened street. While in front of him, as if controlled separately, his hands worked at his bread in furtive tears and twists, dismantling the piece of baguette into smaller and smaller bits until there was nothing for his fingertips to grasp at all. Just crumbs. And his fingers went limp and trembling, his voice trailed off.

Catherine thought she knew exactly what he meant.

His eyes returned to hers, the nick in his iris catching mercury street light. He straightened, adjusting his position in the chair minutely so that he was returned all at once to some elegant balance that she understood to be a matter of surfaces and projections as opposed to what was real.

"In the water, I was lucky to get a hold of some floating debris. That's where they found me," he said. "I was in the hospital for six weeks. Collapsed lung, right side. Both ankles broken."

Her throat was dry, listening. Rostock too was still drifting.

"I was in the water a long time," he said. "It was terrible."

"I know," she whispered.

"More people might have lived if it hadn't been for the fires."

Catherine doubted that, but was now frozen remembering. Explosions and an eerie absence of cries for help. A section of the tail sinking from view in the shining black bay. Flames licking across the surface of the water, heads bobbing and disappearing. Seat cushions, carry-on luggage, a dog kennel. Catherine herself blinking to life, one arm draped over a piece of wreckage, realizing that she had somehow been washed up close enough to shore that she could stand.

"I'm sorry," Rostock said, seeing her expression.

Catherine clenched her jaw. Opened and closed her hands. "It's fine," she said, just as appetizers arrived. Sweetbreads, oysters. The waiter said something to each of them about the dishes, but Catherine missed it all. Breathing steadily. Righting herself.

After the hospital, Rostock went on, that's when it really began. When something new was introduced. Some troubling element.

Catherine looked up, waiting.

"Have you heard of identity theft?" Rostock asked.

It was much, much more than the inconvenience, you might imagine. There was something penetrating about this particular crime. Google it, Rostock told her. There was a lot of the modern person wrapped up in what we casually call "identification." Snips of plastic and laminated paper, a constellation of cards and numbers and accounts and PINs that may be reassembled into a powerful proxy. They acted for you, standing in your stead in strange and forceful ways. Rostock felt that most destabilizing of feelings: that a copy of himself had been released into the world and was at that moment beyond his own control.

"Your documents have no real life until they're out of your hands. Then they really do." He picked up an oyster.

You get a call one day from a bank you've never heard of complaining about an overdue account you've never heard of either. In his case, a Citibank Visa card maxed out to its $20,000 limit and unpaid since the original charges, which had been made all over the Midwest and the South.

He assumed a mistake, as everyone did at first. He told Citi they had the wrong Michael Rostock. They came back with a lot of convincing evidence that they had exactly the right man. They had his social security number on file, details from his Illinois Identification Card, a cancelled cheque from an existing account. He called an acquaintance, a man involved in computer security whom Rostock knew from his racquet club. The man gave Rostock his first education on the topic. Identities were stolen and then used to all kinds of ends: to impersonate for criminal purposes, to steal money directly from the person whose identity was involved, to get new documents, new passports, to use those in who knew how many fraudulent ways. A black web of nasty options were branching and spreading in Rostock's mind, shadows flitting and scheming.

Talk to your bank, call the Federal Trade Commission and the FBI.

"And the FBI took a real interest, too," Rostock remembered. "I was pleased. I drove out Roosevelt Road later that same day."

Rostock in a small interview room with table and chairs. And when the agents arrived he wasn't waiting for questions. He told them everything he thought they might conceivably need to know, probably far more. His wife, the fact that he had no kids. The fact that he was one of six survivors of the famous Air France Flight 801.

"They took note of that," Rostock said, looking across the table at Catherine.

"Yes, people do," Catherine said, taking a sip of wine.

Rostock finished his appetizer in silence, then set his fork down. The waiter approached, quietly this time, having noticed the focused intensity of their conversation. He took their empty plates and withdrew.

"They were friendly, these agents," Rostock said. "But when they started in on their own questions, I could feel something change in the room."

They were asking about his work, the exact nature of the research, the partners with whom he collaborated. They were asking about the car he drove and whether he had a Registered Traveller card for travel between the U.S. and the U.K. These questions went on and on, and it was only deep into the second hour that it finally occurred to Rostock that they were less interested in a theoretical third-party identity thief than they were in Rostock himself.

"I was slow on the uptake," Rostock said now, with a sigh.

He remembered the turning point. The moment he realized they were trying to make his answers jibe with some existing theory about other things that had already happened. He stopped talking, mid-sentence. He'd just been explaining in more detail his core research area. He was telling them about the study-in-progress in partnership with Johns Hopkins—two thousand women, double-blind tests, multiple universities involved, high profile, high potential. He'd told them about cancer markers, their potential usefulness relative to the mammogram. He shook his head, recounting to Catherine these details, aware now of how oblivious he'd been, trotting out statistics and describing the impact the work might have.

"I suddenly heard myself talking, volunteering all this information. And I stopped."

What was he doing? He had no criminal history. He'd been a Boy Scout, for crying out loud. A Boy Scout raised by a decorated Second World War hero who had himself gone on to become a well-known District Court judge. They sided with the law, the Rostocks. His uncle had been senior in the NYPD, a detective with awards and famous cases to his credit. His son, Rostock's cousin, was with the FBI himself, a Special Agent in Charge, no less. Rostock and his cousin weren't close, but those were the facts. He was copped-up. He was law-side.

"Mason," Rostock said. "My cousin's name was Mason Hill. SAC Hill. I didn't mention it, because I suddenly realized that they would know. They knew all about me. I had a cousin senior to them. But also everything I'd been telling them, they knew already. My research and reputation."

"So what did you do?" Catherine asked. She felt a certain nervous energy passing through her. Rostock was animated, even agitated. She guessed he didn't get this way often. But she also understood why. There was a familiar sense of mounting pressure in the situation he was describing. She knew a bit about that, mounting pressure and suspicious glances from people who seemed to know as much about you as you did yourself.

Rostock threw himself into their hands. He said he didn't understand what was going on, but he suspected it was more than just his stolen ID and a fraudulently obtained credit card.

They nodded and left the room, then came back fifteen minutes later with a file of papers. Rostock remembered looking at the bulging envelope with a growing sense of emptiness in his chest. A stolen identity induced a certain sense of having lost control. That file, fat with data, hollowed him out.

Catherine heard that. *Hollowed out.* She thought of an empty space that appeared behind her heart. She suppressed the feeling that it might be opening in her now, releasing its flickering images and distracting sensations. She forced herself to listen and said nothing.

The agents produced the picture of a building for Rostock, which they said wasn't that far from where he lived himself in a condominium that had been made by sub-dividing one of those old limestone Hyde Park mansions. Bridgeport, they said, west of Armour Square Park where the White Sox played. None of that meant anything to Rostock. He'd never lived in Bridgeport. He wasn't sure he'd ever been up there.

The agents turned pages. Moved on to other questions. Did he take any prescription medications? Did he have trouble with any colleagues at work? Did he own or possess any firearms? Did he use pornography? Had he recently shaved off a beard?

That last question marked a moment. He said no, because he hadn't. At which point the younger detective produced another photograph and slid it across the table. It was Rostock at the door of the same building they'd just shown him, an innocuous building on an innocuous Bridgeport street. Or, it could have been him, it looked an awful lot like him, only with a beard.

"It wasn't me. I didn't know the place. I'd never worn a beard. I'd never worn the hat the man was wearing."

Catherine was staring at Rostock, the first moment in the conversation when she was forced to consider whether this man might be unspooling. His speech had sharpened and sped up. He was rocking slightly in his chair. His hands kept picking up and setting down his cutlery as if remembering and forgetting what they were doing in an endless, looping cycle. She hadn't been having such a great year herself, but maybe Rostock had come out of the Irish Sea really damaged: invisibly but intractably.

And he had a copy of the photograph with him too. Catherine really didn't want to see it. But he took it from an inside breast pocket and slid it across the table towards her. There it was. She looked up at him and down again at the print. Undeniable.

"All right," she said. "That does look like you with a beard."

"Unsettling," he said.

"I can imagine," she said. But internally she was already reassuring herself. So the guy looked like Rostock. Maybe it was him. Maybe this whole evening was founded on Rostock's delusion. Maybe the dignified Dr. Rostock was nuts.

Mains arrived. Rostock waited until they were on the table and the waiter had again left them. Then he said, "That's when they asked me if I had a lawyer."

He kept sounding sane the moment immediately after Catherine started to wonder otherwise. Now he was tucking into his beef short rib, knife and fork in those elegant hands. He seemed to have calmed entirely. She had to hand it to him as far as dinner companionship went. He certainly wasn't boring.

"So did you?" she said, finally.

Rostock didn't have a lawyer other than the one who'd drafted his long-ago will. But he was panicking. So he rolled the dice and asked if he could talk to his cousin.

Of course, that was a gamble. Pulling rank is always risky. But he was going to try anyway because he'd watched these two for several hours at that point. And Rostock thought he could read at least one thing about them. They were confused. It's a moment of discomfort for medical researchers also: the feeling that your theory is wrong, that you've been over-investing in a wrong approach, a flawed line of inquiry.

"I simply wasn't the guy they were looking for. I wasn't the guy in that photo," Rostock said. "And they knew it."

His cousin called back quite quickly, speaking first to the two agents, and then to Rostock when they passed him the phone and left the interrogation room. "It just isn't me in the photo," he told his cousin.

"Yeah," his cousin said. "I think they're starting to realize that."

Rostock under those winking fluorescent tubes and yellowed paint. He told them he wanted to go. That they would eventually have to release him. *You've changed your card numbers? All passwords have been deleted?*

Rostock said yes, all that had been done.

Another pause. "Okay. Then they're going to release you. And for now, yes: that's it."

Rostock said thanks and goodbye, hung up. Five minutes later he was out on the street driving home, blinking in the bright sunshine, half wondering if he'd imagined the whole thing. It had been a whirlwind of a day, during which his whole life had seemed poised for radical revision. Then it all swung back to normal, but in such a way as to leave the normal slightly askew.

Halfway home, as if to punctuate that sense of things gone strange, his phone rang. Cousin Mason on the line again, this time sounding as though he was calling from outdoors somewhere, like he'd left the office to take a smoke break.

"Sorry about that," Mason said. "Couldn't get into the details right that moment."

"So what is this all about?" Rostock asked.

Well, quite a lot in fact. Turned out the Bridgeport address had been of interest to the police for several months, as it was the location of a computer the Internet activity of which had been under surveillance. Rostock's cousin paused there. Rostock guessed he was smoking.

"Way off the record," his cousin said. "About what your doppelgänger is doing."

Rostock glanced up at Catherine, looking steadily across the table. "You know, it was the first time I'd heard it presented in those terms. *Doppelgänger*. Someone actually out there whose similarity to me was a near-mathematical truth."

Catherine felt a creeping embarrassment. She sympathized. Dr. Rostock had clearly struggled and she knew a thing or two about that. But she realized that she'd agreed to meet Rostock hoping that he might have something for her, something she could really use. And now it seemed that there was only tragedy and madness in his story. And she found herself clearing her throat, taking a long sip of water, thinking of her train back tomorrow and DIY and all that needed tending there.

Rostock was still talking. And his story was getting worse. The computer in Bridgeport had at least one other federal agency taking close notice. Hacking. Online trespass. Data theft. Seemed like the person involved had a special interest in medical databases. The first report, in fact, had come from the system security people at Johns Hopkins where Rostock himself worked.

"You can appreciate," Rostock said, "this news made me most uncomfortable."

Catherine nodded mutely. But she was struggling to decide exactly how much of Rostock's story she could afford to believe, to take on personally, to care about. She realized that her heartbeat was slightly elevated, a lick of anxiety passing through.

"Ever heard of the Deep Web?" Rostock asked her now.

Rostock hadn't either, but his cousin brought him up to speed. The Deep Web was good at black markets: pharmaceuticals, firearms, varieties of pornography. Things people would want to know a respected university medical researcher was buying. His cousin wondered if he knew anyone who had recently acquired a grudge.

"And did you?" Catherine asked.

Not that he knew. So he changed his passwords. He signed the consent for the FBI to search his home. He watched them look through his closets, dust his keyboard for fingerprints, examine his bookshelf, opening books and shaking the pages. Then he watched them leave and he never heard from them again.

Catherine staring, transfixed. Then, seeming to wake. "Well," she said. "What an ordeal."

"And it's wasn't over," Rostock said.

She'd been afraid of that. But she couldn't leave now.

The situation for Rostock was still far from stable, he said. The people at Johns Hopkins were asking hard questions. His own lab had reported data anomalies. Rostock told them about the identity theft, although nothing about the Deep Web activity. People seemed more or less placated, but still the questions were there. And after a couple of weeks, he was officially suspended from the research project. Temporary, everyone said. Just temporary. He decided to retire. Make it easier on everyone.

"I am my reputation," Rostock said. "Professionally speaking, as a researcher, it's my single asset. The thing I'd built over all those years. Someone was targeting that single thing I really owned."

A month passed, two months. Rostock wasn't sleeping. He was using pills, which seemed less and less effective. His cousin had got him a copy of the photograph the agents had shown him. He'd find himself up in the wee hours staring at it, wondering unimaginable things.

"It wasn't even that the guy looked exactly like me," Rostock said. "He didn't. But there was something *of me* in him."

He was questioning his own sanity by this point. Wondering if it were possible that he'd done these things himself. Stolen money from himself. Tried to sabotage his own work. Done awful things online. Was he crazy?

Rostock reached the breaking point standing in his own living room one evening, three in the morning, staring down through the trees and out onto the boulevard. A bottle of sleeping pills in his hand. "I wasn't going to do it," Rostock said, pausing, knife and fork trembling above his plate. "I didn't believe I would ever get to such a place, such despair. But there I was. And there was someone out there, some entity that had turned on me and forced me there."

He didn't know about the others at that point, but he committed in the moment to finding out. Nancy Whittle. Adrian Janic. Patricia Langston. Douglas Marshall. He didn't know yet that all of them were gone already, but he'd soon enough learn the truth. Depression. Paranoia. Isolation. The feeling of being followed. The feeling of having been somehow split in two.

"*I'm following myself. I will catch myself. And then we'll see who wins.* That was Marshall's last statement to the world. The others seem to have experienced something similar."

He went so quickly from frightened to angry, Rostock said. *I will catch myself. Then we'll see who wins.* It was a call to confront, he thought. It was a call to defeat this other being. Move towards the entity. Move towards it and do not let it scare you into silence and inaction.

Catherine was staring at Rostock, hand over her mouth, not trying to hide the fact that she was now concerned. But he didn't notice. He'd gone somewhere outside the room. He was speaking with a quiet urgency, a low intensity of tone, quite unlike his voice when she'd first arrived. He sounded absolutely mad.

"Confront and defeat," Rostock said.

Catherine was feeling the need to slow things down, to stabilize. "I'm not following," she started.

But Rostock couldn't even hear her. You had to enter their place, he was saying. You had to look them in the eyes. You had to threaten them and only then did they disappear.

Catherine was sitting back in her chair, wondering how far this might spiral. "Threaten who?" she said.

So here it came. Rostock had done his research all right. He knew the history. He knew the lore, the variations on the theme. *Doppelgänger. Ankou. Fylgia. Fetch.* In ancient Egypt they called the mystic double the *ka*. In Norse legend it was the *vardøger*. They turned up in Icelandic lore, Russian, Chinese. Virtually all cultures since the beginning of recorded history had spoken of the phenomenon, people who found themselves facing the deadly, ill-willed opposite. The nearly identical evil twin.

"I'm a scientist, Catherine," Rostock said. "You think I don't realize this sounds crazy?"

It sure did, Catherine thought. But it wasn't in the end as crazy as what came next. She listened and felt it like a punch to the solar plexus. It seemed, Rostock said, that theirs was a particular kind of double. *Theirs.* This thing he believed they shared. Theirs was a double spawned at the moment of tragedy when one friend lives and another friend dies. It was the double for survivors. Part of the Celtic tradition, this one: a category of *fetch* known in Gaelic as the *ion dubh*.

"The *ee-on dove*," he said, enunciating the words very carefully, "are black birds."

Her hands were on the edge of the table now, gripping it as if for balance.

"I saw them, Catherine," he said, voice wavering, throat seemingly constricted with emotion. "I was surrounded by them as I fell. Thudding wings and cold bodies. Feathers close. I saw and I felt the *ion dubh*."

Here he waited for her to answer, his eyes expectant, intensely so, wide and shining but for that flaw, a glint of metallic black. And Catherine, whose heart was now pounding so that she thought it must be visible, thudding up through her clothes, sat staring at this stranger, held miserably in that shared moment and memory.

But refusing to be snared. She would not listen to the end of this story. She didn't want to know what confronting, threatening, what defeating meant to Dr. Rostock. She wished intensely that she didn't know any of what he'd told her.

"I think I need to go to the ladies' room," she said. A sudden, urgent necessity, nothing at all to do with needing a toilet.

She left the dining room. Slow steps, she told herself. Do not run. She splashed cold water on her face and looked in the mirror. She retreated to a stall and sat on the closed seat top, eyes closed, pinching the bridge of her nose, concentrating on just that feeling, the central pressure there.

Then she went back into the dining room to find the table empty, the dishes cleared, the bill paid. And Dr. Michael Rostock gone too. Vanished into that frigid Chicago night.

CLOUD GATE

NO ANSWER VAL. NO ANSWER PHIL.

Catherine was in a taxi, eastbound on Lake Street into the heart of the city. She wanted desperately to talk with someone, anyone really with whom she could imagine a trusting closeness. Kalmar came to mind strongly, her now elusive Warehouse mystic, who'd put his hands on her hips, tried to pull her close, but whom she had resisted. Other decisions meant other lives. And in another life she would have heard his voice now, low and soothing in her ear.

She had the taxi stop under the El tracks in the Loop and began walking down State Street, no destination in mind. There were white flurries stirred up by passing traffic, icy puddles in the street. She was forced to step indoors just to take off the biting chill, where she found herself almost immediately overheated. Tropical humidity in the perfume section at Macy's. She felt short of breath and unable to see clearly. Her eyes were dry and her head hurt. So outside she went again, into the blasting, arctic November streets, the sidewalks shooting their concrete chill directly up through her shoes. Down State through the crowds. Jostled at the shoulder, forced to step aside. Loud, bawling groups of people seeming to consist only of goateed men talking far too loudly and large women in Canada Goose parkas, aggressive and unaware.

Catherine was close to visible emotion and angry with herself for it, wheeling finally into Monroe Street, crossing again under the El tracks at Wabash, timed on this occasion to a passing train which thundered overhead, a chaos of metal on metal, the sound of something very large shuddering and dismantling itself into a million constituent bits. The Art Institute was closed. She stood in front of the building, on the steps next to the lions, who'd been seasonally adorned with wreaths of spruce and red ribbons, their pedestals wrapped to look like gift boxes, striped paper and festive bows. There was moisture threatening at the corners of her eyes just as a woman stepped from a cab at the curb, alighting, a theatre-goer, but seeing her clearly. And she was so stung with embarrass-ment to be seen close to tears that she sharply turned her back and walked up Michigan towards Millennium Park, past the looming video pillars of the Crown Fountain, children's faces in LED loops, smiling, laughing, pursing their lips to synch with the water that issued forth from the face of the monoliths at regular intervals. It was possible to be mesmerized by this rotation of citizens on statu-esque display. The children seemed to Catherine as if they wanted to speak and were being constrained across time and distance, whis-pering inaudibly from within the matrix of colour and shape and moving shadows.

In the park there were walkways lined with lights that spiralled up towards the Cloud Gate sculpture, a mirrored aluminum kidney bean that reflected and distorted the city around it, bending the bristling skyline to form a brilliant circle, like an iris around the black pupil of the Chicago nighttime sky. No stars. Never stars in the city, whose own light darkened the heavens, making a black hole into which Catherine found herself staring.

"Would you like me to take your picture?" asked a woman, who stepped just that moment to her elbow.

Catherine started and turned. And though it was irrational to think so, she did think for an instant that this was the same woman who'd watched her earlier, though she'd had no more than a second to even see her features. Catherine never answered. She pushed herself off in the opposite direction instead, a gloved hand to hold her scarf to her face, to hide and warm herself.

Michigan Avenue was flowing. A river of buses and taxis and cars. The light took forever to change and Catherine stood there in the swirling snow as it turned to angling sleet and pulled her coat tighter around her just as her phone began to buzz in her pocket. She snatched it out, gasping, again near tears. Valerie, please. Only it wasn't her sister. Not Phil either. It was a text from Rostock.

I'm sorry. I went too far. Do stay in touch. It's important.

She deleted it angrily. She stepped into the street and crossed. What did he want her to do? She didn't want to know. *Confront and defeat. Enter the place where they live.* It was craziness. She crossed the continent to meet with the proof that all of the other survivors had lost their minds.

She was walking in circles. She'd walked east and then south, then north and west. She was now heading south again, freezing. She'd just pulled up in front of the Chicago Athletic Association, which advertised a rooftop bar and an evening hot toddy special. As she pushed through the revolving door, she found herself looking up the street behind her, scanning the approaching faces for the woman she now thought she might have seen twice before. What had she even looked like? She could hardly pull a detail back. About Catherine's age, fine features, long hair. Reddish? Maybe. She couldn't be sure.

In the elevator there was a p
first bar. They were talkative a
confines of the elevator so tha
instantly, opening her coat nov
the group were talking about c
checking their reflections in the
felt invisible among them. And
tor and into the wide room

Catherine saw that it was filled with groups and pairs of people, heads close over shared plates and steaming drinks.

On the patio outside couples were kissing. She wandered to the railing and stared down and found again the Cloud Gate, crowds gathering around. And as she gripped the railing over those glittering lights below, her eyes drifted out towards the blackened lake, and something seemed to rise in the funnel of darkness, a flickering, shuddering column or cloud, composed she realized suddenly of thousands of individual marks of blackness, a swarm, a cloud, a flock, *a murder*. Black crows in their thousands. The product of a long ago falling and two perplexing, defeating years.

A waitress arrived with a drink, which Catherine did not precisely remember ordering. Hot apple cider with a sluicing of good rum. She felt the warmth taking her, spreading through her limbs. Her phone buzzed again but it did not startle her. She knew who it was. She knew he would press to tell her what he thought he knew. She'd crossed the distance towards him, stepped up onto a pebbly far shore.

Please be careful. I do believe that the danger is real.

In the park below, the children's faces on those video monoliths were elongated by the angle, distorted and mysterious, like distant, silent gods. Catherine thought of the children that had died the day she survived and she pitched forward, leaning out, feeling the cold air rising from the street below. Some static charge had taken her. And her vision adjusted bird-like in response, her eyes narrowing and zooming, and she thought she was able to look right down to the street with clarity, to see a woman standing there, staring up: about Catherine's age, fine features, long red hair. Eyes locked on Catherine's alone.

Catherine on a rooftop staring down. Catherine in a taxi, crossing a river, heading north on Michigan under the glittering towers, the twinkling lights in a thousand trees, the shuddering shadow of a million black birds behind her. The *ion dubh* who had borne her down to the water, slowed her fall, dropping her gently into the Irish Sea. Not unscratched, but only scratched.

In her hotel room she sat cross-legged on the golden textured bedspread, Catherine Bach in possession of some new sense of herself. She had not beaten the past. And she hadn't come to understand the future beyond the fact that she was hurtling into it, and that Morris and Kate Speir now waited in some way for her ahead, a step farther down the trail, around a bend, advanced already some crucial increment towards whatever would ultimately happen.

But she was centring, somehow. And when she heard a knocking at the door, she calmly rose, did not consult the peephole because she knew who it was. Door open. Hallway completely empty.

She was alone.

THREE

"Bow or not? Call back or not? Recognize him or not?" our hero wondered in indescribable anguish, "or pretend that I am not myself, but somebody else strikingly like me, and look as though nothing were the matter. Simply not I, not I—and that's all."

—FYODOR DOSTOYEVSKY, *The Double*

SUBJECTIVE DOUBLE DELUSION

THE RULE OF STEPHENS.

Catherine was reviewing what she knew to be true about the rule. She thought it was worth reminding oneself from time to time, repeating the principles in play, confirming your own deliberate choices. Effects have causes. Dr. Rostock as she encountered him was a curious effect of a cause called AF801. But to have this peculiar effect, AF801 did not have to depend on any kind of Kingsian paranormal aberration. There was a Hawkingsian explanation that Catherine might not yet fully understand, and that gnawed at her still a day after their encounter, but that she was forced to remind herself must be there.

On the train home, Catherine turned her attention to the challenge of her immediate future. Morris's notification was supposed to be confidential for the duration of those thirty days. So all Warehouse eyes would be on her in the ordinarily expectant ways. Thinking about that, Catherine registered that Rostock was also a cause in his own right, which could of course have different effects. She could let it preoccupy her, drive her crazy. But she wasn't going to allow that. She'd had her lifetime quota of crazy in the past two years. It was surely time for a little cold-eyed, Hawkingsian rationalism.

She called Phil from the train. Might as well get things rolling immediately. "So thirty days," she said. "How convenient of Morris to bring this whole thing to a head the week before Christmas."

"Twenty-nine days," Phil said. "But I'm glad you're counting."

"My big announcement," she said. Then she told him. On her return to Vancouver, they were going to go straight to feature testing. Two hundred human subjects. They were going to prove out the technology and push towards beta release.

"Whoa," he said.

"Hasn't Morris been telling me to do exactly this, Phil? Telling me I'm stalling? Telling me I brought Mako on myself?"

"Yeah, okay." Phil sounded genuinely confused. "But I never thought you were stalling. I thought you had technical reasons for thinking the test was too soon. All that's suddenly changed?" Besides, he said, a two-week test was much shorter than the three or four months she'd been talking about. It was also incredibly short notice for the team to pull off. Her mooring technology wasn't where she wanted it to be. "You told me all these things," Phil said.

"Yeah, I did," Catherine said. "But I'm tired of being blamed for holding things back. And if tests do go well then we'll have great data to justify a beta release and we could be generating revenue inside a year."

Maybe so, Phil was saying. But all that upside would belong to Mako by month end.

Maybe not, Catherine said. Maybe month end would turn out differently than people were assuming.

Catherine was standing in her train suite now, rocking back and forth with the motion of the car, enjoying the sense of herself streaming through the landscape. This was absolutely the only way to go, she was explaining. Because if they killed at test, maybe she could raise the money herself.

"What if the test doesn't go so well?" Phil said.

Well then maybe Mako walks away.

"Or sues you," Phil said. "For rushing it, for forcing the matter, for affecting the results and valuations."

Why was he being so negative? Why wasn't he pleased for her? For the first time in years, Catherine felt a tick of irritation with Phil. Now would be a good time for him to say something encouraging and here he was telling her that a safer bet might be to just hold the course, not try anything too spectacular.

"What does that actually mean, Phil?" she said. "Nothing too spectacular."

She had exactly the spectacular in mind because DIY deserved it. The people who worked there. All those millions of potential users, waiting and pre-registered, longing to regain some kind of control over their own bodies.

"Listen," Phil said, "I admire your energy, your commitment here still, under these circumstances."

There was a pause, during which Catherine heard Phil calculating the countervailing factors. The reasons why her energies were in this situation misplaced or unwise. But then he seemed suddenly to lose energy himself. As if what most crucially had to be said that moment wasn't something that he wanted to be the one to tell her: that she was making this decision in a high-strung state, fuelled by emotions, in denial about some bigger, more looming issue. And putting his finger uncannily close to what that bigger issue just might have been, he then asked her, "So, how was your dinner?"

She sat down suddenly, put her feet up on the other seat. Perhaps in a strange way, dinner had inspired her. Obvious clinical issues aside, Rostock was a survivor. They had that in common. And his intensity in the end might have been subtly infectious. Challenges seemed suddenly best met head-on. Problems demanded action, not capitulation. Perhaps it had been Rostock who'd awoken her to the bloody-mindedness required, which in her case seemed to have been steadily muted over the past two years.

She didn't tell Phil any of that. She saw that going forward he couldn't be expected to be there for her in quite the same way as before. So she said very little. Dinner had gone fine. Old friend, good to catch up. She suggested lunch sometime after her return, after she got the test up and running. In the meantime she had many more calls to make. She had to get going.

"Safe travels," Phil said quietly. "Please take care of yourself."

Twilight. The train was hurtling through the northernmost Chicago suburbs now, stations flashing by in the lowering sun. But still afternoon in Vancouver and the Warehouse would be buzzing. So she signed off with Phil on that faintly sorrowful note and started to work the phone. That evening. First thing the next morning and all through that day. She activated the team, gave them each their task lists, fielded questions. Yohai, crucially. He was going to have to build out the prototype *Red Pill 2.0* at long last, getting those diagnostic modules and the mooring tech loaded as best they could. Functionality would still be limited, Catherine had decided, poring over the data with Yohai on their separate screens, connected in phone space as she bounced across Montana. They'd build in the base suite of vital stats. They had stable test data for the diagnostic modules on gout, diabetes, hep A, malaria and cirrhosis. Catherine thought user experience, the website, expert advice feedback could all be tested in later rounds. So Hapok and Kalmar could take a back seat during this phase. They all met in a final conference call as Catherine crossed the Continental Divide going westward. And by the time she got to the Warehouse the next morning—two and a half days after making the decision to go—they had the test online, subjects recruited through the lab, the *Red Pill 2.0* swallowed and moored and monitors in place. Two weeks of real data and they would know something about DIYagnosis that they had not been able to know before. They'd have a glimpse of their own future.

"Nervous?" Yohai said at his desk, watching the first data sets flow in and collate. User profiles and the dense matrix of numbers signalled their activity within.

Catherine stood at his shoulder. "What could possibly go wrong?" she asked. And here she lifted her eyes to find them locked immediately with Kalmar's, on the far side of the Warehouse. He'd been looking at her steadily, and now nodded a slow greeting from where he stood, raising three fingers to his temple in a Cub salute.

"Well it could not work, for example," Yohai said. "We are pushing it here."

"So far, so good," Catherine said, looking at those profiles populating with data on the screen.

"The mooring could fail," Yohai said, deadpan. "These screens could go blank any second."

"All right, all right," Catherine said. "I'll leave you alone."

Yohai grinned just as Hapok arrived at the workstation. He put his hand on Catherine's shoulder. He never really smiled, as Mr. Clean himself might have under the circumstances. But he shook her hand solemnly and nodded his head. She felt the bulk of him in that shake, his enormous arms. "Good luck, boss," he said.

"Hey, you too," she said. Though the expression on his face as he withdrew indicated that her need was the greater.

Catherine returned to her own workstation. She knew she couldn't hover over Yohai, who was probably going to sleep at his computer for the next two weeks. As for her, the bet was down. The croupier had spun the wheel. The ball was in the track where it would spin for a while before the drop. Tense, sure. But also a hovering sense that not much more could immediately be done. Catherine felt passingly weightless. Though only briefly, as she spied intern Arwen just then and waved her over. There were, of course, other outstanding matters that needed to be resolved.

They walked outside for the few moments they spoke. Arwen was wearing a denim shirt pulled over a T-shirt with a picture of a large, anatomically correct brain. Text: *The Brain*. Curly long dark hair. Thin, intelligent face. A special assignment, Catherine told her. It would only take her a day or two and maybe a trip to the library.

Arwen was looking at Catherine intently as she spoke. The assignment had an unusual shape and the young woman seemed to relish the opportunity.

She went to see Valerie at her shop a few days later. Valerie had been phoning since Catherine got back from Chicago. Catherine hadn't had a minute to think and then—Yohai hunched over his screens with her own number on speed dial—it was clear she could afford the time for a coffee.

"Take a day," Yohai had said to her. "Take two. I'll call you with anything big."

"I don't know," she said.

"I'll be honest," Yohai said, not looking up, eyes still on his screen. "You're kind of making me tense."

Valerie gave her a sisterly hug full of all her typical compassion and concern. The shop had been decked out for Christmas and looked very Valerie, Catherine thought, noting the silvery green ornaments and dusty blue vases with dried flowers. Pine cones and lichen strewn on the painted tables. Folded piles of printed textiles and racks of craft bath products, tubes of hand cream. Her sister's touch was evident everywhere. And the shop was bustling too. Valerie had to stop and chat with customers several times just on the way to the door.

In the coffee shop next door Catherine told Valerie about Chicago, starting with her meeting with Morris. She felt herself rushing a bit through it, not sure she really had the time to dwell, but on the other hand telling Valerie because telling Valerie anything over the years had been an opportunity for them to mutually check and balance one another. They needed each other's opposing tendencies and understood it without having to discuss the dynamic. Valerie's flair and emotion, her passion for expression. Catherine's pragmatism, or whatever it was that Catherine had always had. Catherine could well see that in the past year the dynamic might have shifted slightly with all her own volatility. And for the first time, visiting Valerie in her busy shop impressed on Catherine not just her sister's passion and dramatic flair, but the reservoirs of common sense, the stable sense of the world and the future that were also reflected. She ran the show well in genteel West Vancouver, in the shop and in her home. Valerie's was not a flaky success.

And when Catherine finished describing her meeting with Morris, Valerie confirmed that impression. "You know what I say," her sister told her. "I say you go talk to Mako directly. Show them who you are. Maybe they'll see the light, buy out Morris and work with you."

Maybe that was a better idea than simply hoping that the *Red Pill 2.0* test would impress so much that Mako would change their mind. It was proactive and Catherine appreciated that. The only problem was that Mako was hidden behind veils of secrecy. Kate Speir. Based in Seattle. That's all she had.

"Mark might be able to find out," Valerie said. "It's all degrees of seperation with tech fund people."

So Catherine agreed Valerie could make a discreet inquiry. Then she went on to the story of Dr. Rostock, who had continued to text her with vague warnings and pleas that they stay in touch. Catherine had been ignoring these, not feeling she could afford to let his madness get too close. But she didn't tell Valerie all those details. She stayed on the dinner instead, the story he told. As she spoke, Catherine could see a furrow working its way in between Valerie's eyes. And by the time she got to her bathroom exit, her return to find Rostock gone, her sister's expression had migrated to one that Catherine remembered from over the years. A look of glazed wonder. A trace of something childish, a wish that the world might yet have magic in it.

Catherine, in observing this, felt herself adopt the old role, as if in that classroom so long ago.

"It was identity theft, Valerie," Catherine said. "That's all it was."

"But all that other stuff he told you."

"Oh, he was messed up by the experience, which I can understand. Terrible situation."

"What about the other passengers?" Valerie said. "None of that happened?"

"Not *none* of it," Catherine acknowledged. "The suicides were real."

Here Arwen had carried out her special assignment quite brilliantly. A research job. She didn't phone the families, of course. But she tracked down the obits, which all, in the end, had a particular kind of language. Never *suicide*. But words like *tragic, untimely. An end to the suffering. After a short illness.* It was easy enough to read between those lines, even if it didn't get you to the *vardøger* or the *ion dubh* or whatever Rostock thought had been coaxed up out of the depths in those moments on the Irish Sea.

"Plus there is the whole head injury aspect," Catherine said.

Arwen again. Delusional Misidentification Syndrome. It was well covered in the peer-reviewed literature.

Catherine realized she'd grown oddly agitated trying to discuss these things. And she looked away, fanning herself with a paper napkin. The coffee shop was filled with tables. It seemed to Catherine that at every one of them two women of about their own age were leaned in together over biscotti and Americanos, telling stories, checking in with each other, listening so hard.

"Delusional Misidentification Syndrome," Valerie was saying, holding her own coffee in both hands, sipping, peering over the rim.

"Exactly," Catherine said. "So, you ever find yourself thinking that Mark has been replaced by an identical imposter?"

"There was this time he lit candles that ran all the way up the stairs and into the bedroom. That was before the kids, clearly."

"Well, if you thought that he was inhabited by an imposter, and you thought that seriously for any length of time, then you would be suffering from what is known as the Capgras Delusion."

Valerie and Catherine exchanged a look.

"Nope," Valerie said. "Pretty sure he's still him."

"Of course you are," Catherine said. "Fregoli Delusion?"

"I give up."

That was when you thought different people you met were actually the same person in disguise. Then there was Inter-metamorphosis, in which the person thought those around them were swapping identities while maintaining the same appearance.

"I sometimes feel that way about the kids," Valerie said.

"No you don't. You don't have a brain injury."

"So what? You have one dinner with the guy, have an intern do a Wiki search and now you're an expert?"

Catherine smiled and adjusted her position in the chair. Arwen and Catherine had done a bit more than that. They'd tracked down a neurologist at the University of British Columbia who specialized in personality and mood disorders in people who have suffered head trauma.

"Well," Valerie said, "she certainly sounds like an expert."

She was indeed. And there was little doubt in her opinion on the topic of what was ailing Michael Rostock. An event killing 499 people involving a still-unexplained explosion and a rapid descent from 28,000 feet at 900 kilometres an hour to sea level at zero—she explained to Catherine, methodically and without judgment—that sort of thing would almost certainly produce a behaviour-altering brain injury or two.

"Or two," Valerie said.

"I'm good, thanks," Catherine said. Point being, Rostock's symptoms were consistent. Mood swings, paranoia. Even the doubling delusion was right out of the diagnostic manuals.

"Textbook," Catherine said to her sister, whose eyes were still on her, but whose mind had clearly drifted to some new concern.

"What?" Catherine said. "Ask."

"What he said about the *ion dubh*," her sister said. "If you're me, that part remains very strange."

Perhaps she shouldn't have told her sister that part. "I don't really know what to say about that," she said to Val.

"Well you could start by telling me if it happened to you," Val said. "Did you see black birds?"

Valerie waited, a look of concern on her features. Her coffee now forgotten on the table between them.

Catherine found herself looking around the busy room again. Eyes to the front window. Of course she'd been haunted now for two years by that precise image, birds in their hundreds, thudding and close. But her heart was not pounding this time, thinking of it. Because if Rostock coming unwound over dinner and afterwards had convinced her of anything, it was that those birds could not in any way harm her. And as a new and odd feature of her own brain chemistry, maybe they would eventually have an opposite and positive effect.

"No, I didn't," she said to her sister, in a lie that she knew was untraceable and unchallengeable however many crows she just now observed to sweep through the trees in the park across the street. Valerie sitting back, looking at her. Valerie still with questions but holding them close to her chest for now.

Catherine back in the car. Driving, driving, driving. The trees in Stanley Park blurring by. She felt her heart beating. She felt her hands gripping the wheel, her legs vibrating on the pedals as the car's tires sang down the pavement.

Know your body. Change your world.

Phil called the day they wrapped the test. He didn't say it directly but Catherine knew why he was in touch again. She was now just twelve days out on the heaviest deadline she'd ever faced and probably ever would face. And yes, there was one way of reading the situation that would lead an observer to think she was ignoring reality. But what a way to ignore reality for two whole weeks.

Your body talks. We'll help you listen.

"Busy?" he said.

She was glad to hear from him, she realized. The conversation on the train was one that might have preceded a long period of leaving each other alone. He couldn't be her lawyer any more, after all. But she was glad to know that in the middle of his afternoon, he might still occasionally pick up the phone to call her as a friend.

"Cone of silence?" Catherine asked him.

"Always."

She was brimming with excitement, which she now allowed him to hear. It was early days. And the test was admittedly short. Hard data hadn't yet even been completely analyzed. And qualitative data from the test participants was yet to come.

"Tell me, Cate," Phil said.

Early word she was getting from the research folks and from Yohai was all positive. They'd gone down huge. The device worked. Subjects seemed to love it. There was still so much more to be done. So much more that the device would soon be able to do. So much more that they all had to offer. But as a base technology, they were there. And if you wanted the potential to track seven risk factors for Alzheimer's, to know if your mitochondria were emanating a pulse of something troublesome, a whiff of malignancy in the germinal works, well then DIYagnosis had a device you could swallow, a dashboard you could load onto your phone, an interface with experts that was robust and reliable for a very reasonable fee.

"Catherine," Phil said. And he let the line run silent.

She was rocking back and forth at her desk. She was biting her lip, smiling.

"Thrilled," Phil said finally. "Absolutely thrilled. You did it. You really did."

A prince among men, she thought. Phil didn't say a word about deadlines or the fact that what she had accomplished might belong to someone else in twelve short days. There was no point and he realized it. She'd done this madly and would see where it went. He only made her agree to lunch that Friday. A celebration was required no matter what happened. She agreed and hung up, her eyes were drifting around the Warehouse now. Things normal enough, things buzzing almost as usual. Almost, Catherine thought, as they had before AF801 had changed things so utterly. Fingers on keyboards and low conversations, people in twos and threes along the counter in the canteen. Someone pulling together picnic tables for a management meeting she'd called herself. Everyone seemingly still in the envelope of not knowing enough to wonder if it all was about to change.

She wanted to believe that. She wanted to believe what Phil had told her back in Chicago. That Mako would want things quiet. And that Morris would do whatever he had been told. But in front of her managers, having gathered them there to share great news, it was impossible not to sense some other presence in the room. Some invasive sentiment. They sat at those picnic tables with their teams. Yohai had his two lead engineers. Hapok and Kalmar with their people. They wanted to be excited for the news that they all of course knew was coming. But some vague worry held them back.

Catherine, who was never long on procedure, dove right in. "Dudes, we crushed it."

There was a quiet *whoot* from the back of the room, and some hesitant smiles did appear. And when Yohai took the lead citing numbers, things lightened further. The mooring had worked. They'd deactivated the power source and the devices had flushed. Someone made a crude joke and people laughed. And Catherine sat back, relieved, but feeling the restraint.

"Design feedback?" Hapok speaking from the far end of the tables. "I sent you materials."

Catherine walked through the longer test schedule. *Red Pill 2.0* tests had focused on the device, on the technology. User experience would be built into the next round. And Hapok listened with his arms folded. "I guess I'm just wondering how design is supposed to respond to user input so late in the game, since it seems we're pressing for release."

Catherine noted his serious expression as always. But fair point. Nobody wanted their last crucial changes made right before going to market. But they weren't quite there yet, she said. And everybody would have time to complete changes. Everybody would be supported in making the product the best it could be. And everybody would be kept in the loop, as best she could. Starting immediately.

Kalmar was tracking her with his eyes as she spoke.

"Any other impending changes we should know about?" Hapok still, those arms folded, biceps bulging.

He may have meant nothing. He may have been fishing for an answer to a question he was not quite yet bold enough to ask. Still, the question did not sit well with her. And as the meeting tables cleared, Catherine remained sitting, absorbing the moment and unsure what the next thing was that she should do. Kalmar, a table away, likewise did not rise. They exchanged a glance. She thought of how long it had been since they'd spoken alone together. She missed him, a wayward feeling. It wasn't what she wanted to feel, but there it was.

"Coffee?" he said to her. And she felt an undeniable surge of pleasure on hearing the request.

They got coffees from the canteen and walked outside, through the railyard warehouses to Main Street, from there past the SkyTrain and across the grass north of the Science Centre's geodesic dome. It had been raining earlier. But the clouds had broken and the shadows had sharpened. There was a crispness in the air along the seawall that traced the perimeter of False Creek, and they headed south and down into the new neighbourhood that had sprung up there: glass condominium complexes with aluminum and wood accents, huge bollards on the walkway, a nod to the area's maritime history. A full-colour sculpture of two enormous sparrows in the main square that Catherine loved for being whimsical and because the DIY Warehouse had its own resident sparrows.

They talked about user registrations for a while. Kalmar gave her the stats, which netted out to the reality that when they opened for business, they might well be swamped. But then he stopped talking, and he chuckled, staring up at the birds.

"Swamped," he said. "Makes me think of something. You know about this sculpture?"

He was gesturing with the coffee cup in his hand. And when Catherine shook her head, he told her. The artist had intended to dramatize the hostile virility of the introduced species. The sparrow was brought from Europe to New York in the mid-nineteenth century, probably because farmers wanted them to control agricultural pests. Didn't work out exactly. They liked cities, it seemed. And since they had the evolutionary advantage of not migrating, they were able to take the best nesting sites before native birds returned from the south each spring.

"We feed them crumbs in the café, yeah? But then they take over nests and kill chicks in their shells."

"I really enjoyed this piece better before I knew that," Catherine said.

"No, no," Kalmar said. "I'm making a point."

All new technologies were invasive species, in their own way. They all displaced. They all killed some part of what came before. But you either believed in the future or you lived in the past. You either advanced or fell back.

"I feel fairly sure that metaphor is flawed, somehow," Catherine said. "But your point?"

Grow or die, Kalmar said. He had nothing against chickadees or robins or swallows. But you had to appreciate that this new neighbourhood—the shiny buildings, the café opposite with that fantastic crusty bread, this very sculpture and the implied statement of what it might represent—could not exist were it not for the aggressive, expansive impulse of the invasive species itself.

None of this exists but for that which once wished to destroy it.

They walked back, a long silent stretch. Kalmar was not typically so philosophical. And Catherine pondered his words, wondering what all he might know. Yet still she appreciated this new candour from him, the implication that a connection was still possible between them, the subtle push that he was giving her without perhaps being fully aware. And a block short of the Warehouse, as if to prove out these impressions, Kalmar put out a hand to stop her. There on the corner near a tire store, they turned to look at each other. His blue eyes steady in hers.

"We're all proud of you," he said. "Don't worry about nobody fist-bumping or high-fiving or whatever. People are proud. I'm proud."

She nodded, not quite sure what to say. But there was more.

"I owe you an apology," Kalmar said. His expression was serious but entirely certain. He'd thought about this next part. "For the night we went to dinner."

"Don't say anything," she said.

"I'm not apologizing for feelings," he said. "Only that I should have known better."

She took a breath. "Me too," she said.

Catherine was not a hugger, but she accepted one now. It was warm and full, and it smelled of leather, wool and a trace of lilac.

Back to work. Back with something like a new spring in her step. She didn't need Kalmar to give her confidence in herself. She didn't need the sparrows to give her permission to fight on, even though the sight of five or six of them just then flitting to a far roost on a rafter high above did make her smile. But the feeling was there. And it was a feeling that she carried back to her workstation, back to her task list, as she refocused on all those things that must come next, as she descended back into the maelstrom of work in the midst of what might be the most important phase of DIY's history, thinking: there might yet be a way that I outplay Morris with my week plus a few days remaining.

Or at least that's what occupied her mind until she caught the intern Arwen looking at her from way across the room, peeking out from behind her monitor in a quadrant of the space the kids called Furry Land for the proliferation of stuffed animals—pandas, cheetahs, a big pink elephant—contributed by who knows who and perched all along the window ledges and even some of the high steel roof members.

Catherine smiled and nodded. Arwen looked as though she'd been caught doing something and waved, slightly manic. Then, realizing how ridiculous that looked, she stood and shrugged. Sat down again.

She crossed the space to Arwen's workstation. She peered over the monitor. "Real quick," she said, motioning with her head that Arwen should follow. They went out past the front desk again and the wall where everybody hung their bikes, out onto the street. The breeze was up. Catherine pulled her coat around her and stood for a few seconds, thinking.

"So the head injury research, great work," Catherine said. "Something else."

"For sure," Arwen said. "Point me and I'll shoot."

Catherine had a business card in her hand. It was her own, which she found she hardly ever used. But on the back of it she'd written another name. All caps. Thin black sharpie.

"Kate Speir," Arwen read aloud, voice and expression blank.

And Catherine thought she knew Arwen well enough at that point
to know the expression would not be simulated.

"Okay," Catherine said. And then she gave Arwen the second
assignment to be kept strictly between them. Anything she could
find out about this person. Any information at all. But absolutely
discreet. And she gave Arwen some numbers to call. People who
might be followed for clues.

"All right," Arwen said, nodding. "I got this."

"And not a word . . ."

"It's in the vault."

"All right then," Catherine said, after a pause, a big sigh. "So . . .
rumours?"

Arwen froze.

"As in are you hearing anything?" Catherine went on. "About
DIY? About the future?"

"Some," Arwen said, voice tight.

"Can I guess and you just nod?"

Arwen was still seemingly frozen. But she did manage a very
small nod.

"Rumours I'm getting married."

Arwen's eyebrows shot up. She shook her head.

"Testing," Catherine said. "Takeover rumours."

Arwen didn't move a muscle.

"Right," Catherine said.

Arwen, blurting it out, finally. "Nobody is for it. But guys can
be real assholes sometimes."

"The Cheryl Tiegs fan club is betting on anybody over the chick
CEO?"

Arwen made a face. Roughly that. And just the guys in the pit,
she said. Nobody in any position of authority had said a word.

"Any of them talking about who it is?"

Arwen said no. Just that someone was taking a run.

"All right," Catherine said. Arwen clearly didn't want to say anything further. So Catherine changed the subject. "What are you working on?"

She was teamed with Hapok in creative. They were developing look/feel palettes and templates for the new website, trying to get somewhere into the zone of a medical procedural but without actually looking like a television show.

"I want you to come on as a designer," Catherine said.

Arwen's hands came out of her pockets and Catherine could see that she wore an antique ring, silver with a ruby. She felt quietly certain that this came from Arwen's grandmother, without feeling the need to ask and confirm.

"Tell Hapok I said so. He'll plug you into Kali to draw up a contract. Tell anyone who needs to they can call me about it. But they don't have to."

And don't sweat the rumours, she said after Arwen had given her a hug. It was going to play out the way it was going to play out. The project remained. DIY wasn't going anywhere. Business as usual. And if Kalmar knew, Catherine thought, she would not ask him to clarify either. *Grow or die.* Kali's comment made more sense by the minute.

But even that was a passing thought, because she was already in the Car-2-Go by that point, heading downtown to the next crucial thing that had to happen. Just keep on pushing and refusing to bend. Hardly more than a week to go. And that was the sum total of her plan.

STEPHANIE GORMAN

THE MEETING WITH THE LAWYER Phil had recommended— Stephanie Gorman, who specialized in commercial disputes—did not in fact go quite as imagined in Catherine's best-case scenario. Best case, Gorman dropped everything and locked up Morris and Mako in innovative lawsuits that made Speir run for the hills. As it actually played out, Catherine felt her situation grow yet more complicated.

They met in Gorman's office, which was in a converted old house in Southeast False Creek, with a view out the window of a neatly trimmed hedge. From the moment she sat down, Catherine picked up that tenuous mix of curiosity and fear that survivors occasionally elicit from strangers. It was analogous to survivor's guilt, on which Catherine had done arguably too much online reading. If you thought you didn't deserve your survival, it was torment. But that same will to balance, to fair gamesmanship, existed in the mind of those you encountered on your return. In the literature, Catherine learned that combat veterans frequently encountered the phenomenon, the perplexed contemplation of those in the community around them who could neither connect to the experience that had been endured and survived, nor crunch the existential calculus that gave rise to the death of one and the sparing of another. She hadn't seen combat. But her experience had left her with a similar psychological endowment. She couldn't imagine any greater fear than what she remembered of that terrible descent. And her experience had also marked her for all to see and wonder about and handle gingerly in their imaginations.

Gorman was a slight, grey-haired woman, perhaps sixty, with a wry intelligence in her unwavering gaze. She wore a grey dress in a soft fabric that elegantly sheathed her narrow frame and a necklace of strung wooden beads in autumnal colours. She shook Catherine's hand firmly and showed her into the boardroom, set up in what must have been the dining room when the place was a family home. There were file cabinets and a wall of legal texts. The table was old but the chairs were modern, high-tech, with fine-mesh black webbing and brushed-steel casters. For the first few minutes of the conversation, Catherine didn't catch it. But eventually she did. The woman, who was on the clock, charging by the ten-minute interval, was failing to square up on the core question and was instead inquiring about Catherine herself, as if Catherine herself were the issue.

"I just want to be clear that there is no allegation relating to my performance in all of this," Catherine said.

"They'd be unlikely to say that directly, no," Gorman agreed.

"Morris triggered the buy-sell because of a disagreement over the pace of development."

"Yes, I understand there were delays," Gorman said.

"We weren't delayed," Catherine said. "We had to reschedule a prototype test date."

"Were there deadlines from Morris that weren't met?"

Morris wasn't in any position to set deadlines, Catherine explained. They were equal-equity partners with no formal provision for who had operational final word, but an informal understanding that Morris would watch the burn rate and Catherine would guide the company otherwise.

"He was the money," Catherine said. "I was everything else."

"Understood," Gorman said. "So then, pace of development."

Catherine explained. Morris had been pushing to test a prototype that wasn't worth testing. "It had virtually no features we'd ultimately be selling," Catherine said. "I considered it a useless exercise." And while that version of events wasn't entirely false, Catherine did feel self-conscious giving that answer. *Fleet of foot means moving now.* That had been her talking in the earliest days, before AF801, before Morris was even on the scene or in her mind. Even back from Chicago and testing the more developed prototype as they'd managed to do, *fleet of foot* was not the phrase Catherine would have used. *Scrambling* was more like it. In her own case also: *desperate.*

Of course, Gorman hadn't known Catherine before. And perhaps this lawyer, as smart as Catherine was starting to think she was, didn't have to have any of this explained to her.

"Perhaps the bigger point," Catherine said, wanting somehow to move on, "is that Morris thought our disagreement over the prototype was enough to trigger the buy-sell. I argue that the dispute was over a routine product development issue, which is insufficient to justify the trigger. So I guess you could say that what Morris and I are disagreeing about is really what kind of disagreement we had."

Catherine thought she had probably been speaking a little too quickly and loudly saying that last bit, which in the end might not even be relevant as she wasn't aware that Morris even needed to establish grounds. She paused. She sipped a glass of water. Gorman took a note or two on a yellow legal pad.

Gorman, finally: "Did you take time off after the accident?"

"Does that matter?"

"Better to think about it now and be prepared."

Sure, yes. She'd taken time off. Two weeks immediately afterwards.

A crow flew into the tree outside the window. Catherine swivelled her chair to take it out of her line of sight.

"Did you talk to a therapist?" Gorman asked. "Take prescription meds at all?"

Catherine found herself revising her assessment of Gorman. She wasn't just being curious and perplexed about AF801. She was wondering how it might be played by another attorney in court, how it could be played against Catherine herself. The damaged survivor. Gorman was doing her job.

"You're thinking they go after my competence in court. Mental well-being, et cetera."

"It's what I'd do if I were acting for them and you sued," Gorman said.

"But they have nothing."

"If they could show ways in which you imposed costs on them," Gorman said, "then I'm afraid they would have something."

"So what are my defences?" Catherine asked.

"Option one," Gorman said. "Raise the money. Buy him out."

Well sure. Catherine told Gorman she had a meeting with bankers that very afternoon. But she had to be realistic about her chances there. "What about I challenge the buy-sell, say I was coerced to sign?"

Gorman shrugged. Sure, you could try that.

"What about I go ahead and release a beta to market," Catherine said. "Add value. File for some new patent. Register the patent in my name personally. Basically lock myself into this somehow?"

Gorman didn't think any of that would hold. And if Morris challenged and won, Catherine would just end up handing him more than he even paid for.

Catherine felt suddenly weary. Her eyes drifted to the window, then sharply back to Gorman. Two crows now.

"So you're saying I'm stuck," Catherine said. "I'm cornered."

Gorman suggested they look at it a slightly different way. "Did you talk about the accident much? To Morris, anyone?"

Catherine closed her eyes very briefly. Then open. "Not at all. Not my sister. Not Morris or Phil. God knows none of the guys at the Warehouse. Well, Kalmar a bit."

Gorman raised her chin, acknowledging the last comment.

"My markets director."

Gorman was still looking at her, waiting.

"We get along, I guess," Catherine said. Then hearing how her own intonation made that sound like a question, she corrected: "We get along. I trust him. We've had personal conversations, not a lot lately. But yes, I told him some of it."

Gorman didn't press. "And other than him?"

"Let's just say that a woman running a development team has enough challenges without advertising her private fears and anxieties. The guys like you much better if you tough it out. Well, some of them do. Others like you less. It's no-win."

"And that is true in fields beyond tech development, I can assure you."

"Of course," Catherine said. "I'm sure."

"What I'm trying to determine here with my perhaps slightly personal line of questioning," Gorman said, steadily, "is what exactly you've been toughing out such that Morris might use this information if it were in his possession."

"Right," Catherine said. "Okay."

Gorman put her pencil down, hands folded again in her lap.

"Then I'll tell you a few things I haven't discussed with many people," Catherine said. And to her own surprise, she made it all the way through without omitting very much at all. The explosion and the descent. A vivid hallucination, crows in their thousands, seeming to come from within her. She described her light injuries, her quick physical recovery. A year of mostly normal followed by a year gone strange. A sense of something alive in the world, tracking her and betting against. Rostock too. Catherine told Stephanie Gorman of that phone call late at night. The man she later agreed to meet and the news he bore of the other survivors. The evidence of his own scars, brain injury and delusion.

"He texts me still," Catherine said. "I don't reply. I just can't be part of that."

No tears through any of this. Not even close. Catherine looked evenly at Stephanie Gorman, a lawyer, and told her these things that she had never told anyone else entirely. And Gorman listened, with an almost startling degree of focus, staring at Catherine, who thought just then that perhaps she wasn't there to ask Gorman for legal advice, not really. She was just telling this person—a woman paid for her confidence—about how the world had changed around her. It felt good to do so. And what did it say about her, she wondered, that therapeutic results were only positive after talking to a lawyer?

Gorman was silent, listening. She sat almost motionless until Catherine was finished. Then she quietly ran the numbers for Catherine, as the lawyer saw them. Could Catherine sue? Sure. Would Gorman represent her? Absolutely.

But would she win?

"We'd probably have to prove that Morris maliciously invented the differences between you," Gorman said. "That would be our challenge."

And they could use Catherine's story in getting there, or they could certainly try. They could argue that Morris changed in his attitudes towards her after the crash, that he became more demanding, that he saw differences where he wouldn't have previously, that he became unreasonable and unsupportive, that he drove them to the crossroads for his own purposes. They could argue all those things, and they might even find a judge who on a certain day would agree that they had a point. Only that was not even the biggest challenge they faced.

The biggest challenge was for Catherine to decide what she wanted to be doing over the course of the next five years, the next professional phase of things. She had options. She could fight a lawsuit. She could focus on buying out Morris herself and running the company. She could take the money and move on to something new.

"You seem like a very resolute person," Gorman told her. "But I sense you wavering here. Why is that, do you think?"

Catherine wasn't sure she ever provided an answer to that. Gorman probably only meant her to think about it. She did remember saying goodbye at Gorman's front door. She remembered a firm handshake and Gorman's hand warmly on her elbow.

In the car. A text from Rostock.

Would you be available to speak today? Something is happening here.

Delete. Immediately. She was so pressed, so busy. She didn't have the time or stamina for it.

Five minutes later. *It would be so good to speak. I have something for you.*

She was driving into downtown, sluggish traffic at Main and Terminal under the singing SkyTrain tracks. She'd just put her phone back into her purse and now it was ringing. *Do not call me*, she thought. *Do not start calling me.* But she rooted around for the phone with one hand, changed lanes. Got honked at. Pulled up the caller on speakerphone and it was Kalmar, whose voice she was deeply relieved to hear.

"We're hiring that intern into design?" Kalmar, sounding dubious. "She's been with us less than six months."

"Tell me, Kali," Catherine said, "how long were you an intern before you got a job?"

"*Hire when it hurts*," Kalmar said, reminding her of something she had said herself numerous times. You can't grow just by adding bodies.

"I still believe that. Only I said go on this one and I mean go."

"We can't hire every girl in tech, right? And she's not in tech even. She has a design diploma from a city college in San Diego I've never heard of."

"Woman, Kali. Arwen is a woman. My company, my call. Now I'm heading into a meeting with bankers. So you have something to tell the boys when you get off the phone."

"Roger that, Dr. Bach," Kalmar said. "One other thing."

"Can it wait?"

He had something, Catherine could hear. But she could only carry so much in her head at one time. She was also very tired, very suddenly. So Kalmar let her go and she rode the elevator up the floors of a different tower to face the bankers. It happened in a big boardroom this time that had never had been a dining room. It had old leather chairs and a high view of the harbour. Three jowly men in dark suits entered. They came in and lined up opposite her, one, two, three. She guessed the middle one would speak first and she was right.

"You're kind of my hero, Ms. Bach," he said.

Not this, not now, she thought. But it was their boardroom and it was their money she was asking to borrow. So she did the AF801 dance again for a while, only this time with no sense that they were curious about her survival. All they wanted to know was what made that plane go down.

"Gentlemen, listen," Catherine said, after ten minutes of speculation about electrical fires in the mainframe, the misfiring of a new Russian space-based laser, ISIS, the Levant, Haqqani fringe groups. "9/11 was an inside job, right? That's what they say. You do the math."

They went quiet and sober and their brows arched and wrinkled and furrowed.

"I'm joking," she said. "Or is two years too soon after my own accident for me to joke about it?"

Which had the intended effect of getting them to open the files in front of them, including her PowerPoint deck with the summary of proposed *Red Pill 3.0* changes and improvements, the financials and projections, the market rollout plan. They talked about that for one minute. Two, tops. Then the one on the left cleared his throat. The junior, sandy hair, French cuffs with links that appeared to be tiny ceramic T-bone steaks. He went on to say quite a lot, in fact, much of which could have been mistaken for high and complimentary praise. Great to hear the second prototype tested so well and that all the projections were strong. Awesome rollout plan, he was sure they were going to benefit from a lot of buzz.

"But at the end of the day . . ."

Catherine wincing internally. At the end of the day DIYagnosis Personal Health Systems had no sales history, no cash flow and no realizable assets beyond the patents, which could not themselves be used as loan collateral because their true value was entirely dependent on the success of the rollout.

"Chicken-and-egg situation," the young man said.

Catherine wanted to cradle her head in her arms and close her eyes. She wanted to drift into a dream and wake up very far away from these men.

"And from a banking standpoint," the young man concluded, without even the courtesy to look uncomfortable saying so, "the only way we could try to help you here is with a personal loan."

"He actually fucking said that," she told Phil over the celebration lunch they'd planned for that Friday. "Personal fucking loan. What am I, just out of college?"

Phil was looking at her, amused. "Cate," he said, "you're saying 'fuck' a lot, and quite loudly."

She sat back. Looked around. "Sorry everyone in this restaurant," she said. They were eating Reuben sandwiches in a place a few blocks over from Phil's office.

"So they said no," he said. "At the end of the day."

"That's the thing. They're such wimps, they try to pretend they're not saying no. They try to pretend they're helping out with this personal loan idea, all the while telling me I don't have the assets to secure it. My ideas are brilliant, my company is a rising star, for sure. Absolutely. Everyone around the table is convinced of that. *Had I thought about approaching another source of venture capital?*"

Phil shrugged. "They have a point. Morris isn't the only VC in the world."

Catherine put her sandwich down. "Do I have to explain this? About me and VCs and the likelihood I'll ever *speak* to one again?"

Phil chewed methodically, his big jaw working away. He swallowed and took a sip of ginger beer. Then he said, "I'm about to change the subject, but only slightly. I got a call from your intern, Arwen."

"She's a design assistant now, in fact," Catherine said.

"Not calling about design, though."

"Yes, was meaning to mention that."

"She said you'd instructed her to make discreet inquiries about Kate Speir."

"Well, I did say that," Catherine admitted. "So what did she ask?"

"She wondered if I could confirm where Mako was based," Phil said. He ate a few fries.

"And you're wondering why I would think you'd ever tell her something you wouldn't tell me."

No, that wasn't it. Catherine might be pushing this inquiry away from herself. Giving it to someone she trusted. "And though it's highly irregular, on a human level, I do get it."

"Well, thanks for that, Phil," Catherine said.

He held up a hand. He smiled. He understood. He specialized in always understanding. "A detail. And this was news to me."

Catherine waited for it.

"They're not in Seattle, or not any more. Not sure how this came about but they've apparently moved to Vancouver. I told your assistant and she's now working on an address."

"Vancouver," Catherine said.

"Seems so," Phil confirmed. "But listen closely here, Cate. If you contact them, it's none of my business and you never spoke to me."

Phil finished his sandwich and smiled at her. Tapped his watch. He leaned across the narrow table for a kiss on the cheek. She watched him make his way up Hastings, westbound towards the glass towers. Big, confident strides. The detail obviously didn't strike Phil as important, even if he could see in her eyes how it was to her. Money was borderless. It had no location. So he went back to work without a thought. And perhaps Catherine should have done the same. Catherine with a week remaining on that ticking clock. But she could not deny the way this one detail, this one bit of news sat with her. It wasn't about Mako Equity any more. It was about Kate Speir. Speir in Vancouver. Speir close at hand. Speir closing the distance, hemming her in. Here was a person with an iron will about her, a cold gaze and a laser focus. And to Catherine it seemed so clear in those moments that this gaze and focus had now fallen on her.

Catherine was in the car, driving rather faster than she normally did. And entirely in the wrong direction. She needed to get back to work. The storm was rising, not levelling off. Seven days, and she had thinking to do, planning and strategizing. She too could muster an iron will. She could do the cold gaze and the laser focus. Circumstances now demanded it, even if she had no firm idea what exactly came next.

But she didn't go back to work just then. She drove north instead, across the Lion's Gate Bridge, up and up towards the looming blue-green mountains, towards the snowcaps and the perspective that she might gain by being there. She drove all the way up the Capilano Canyon to the big parking lot at the foot of Grouse Mountain. Then she paid for her ticket up on the gondola, standing with the crowds of kids heading to ski school, everybody's breath making ghosts as they were cabled up over the towers in that big swinging car.

At the top she rubbed her hands briskly together in the icy chill. She heard the snow squeak under her boots, which were not snow boots, and which sunk awkwardly into the hardpack. She made her way to the wooden walkway, and from there back towards the brow of the hill, to the chalet. She was 1,200 metres above the crisp blue sea, a sign on the open observation deck informed her. And she stood with a coffee at the rail, icicles hanging from the eaves and a brilliant, porcelain blue sky doming overhead. The sun was a white hole in the western quadrant, not yet dropping, seeming as if it might never drop.

This was her city. The glistening glass of the downtown core, the cold inlets, the shipping terminals, those towering orange cranes. The slender bridges spanning the water. In the distance, the green thumb of Point Grey and the UBC campus where they would be, very soon, doing tests on the *Red Pill 3.0* that she and her team had made possible. This was the place where she had put down roots that she had intended to nurture and make into a splendid thing, with branches that would reach to the sky.

What had Morris once told her, from the crow's nest height of his own mahogany boardroom? *Miracles, mystery and juice.* The conquering powers. The fuel for a Promethean will. *Red Pill 3.0* would be the miracle. And if Mako proved anything, it was that there would always be enough available juice.

The sun was making prism colours in the icicles, and casting around itself an enormous ring that fizzed with its own iridescence. Catherine breathed the clear, cool air and thought about the mystery Morris had proposed, a partnership that made no sense on paper, that people might question and criticize, but that would have in it the seeds of something powerful and enduring.

He'd been speaking of himself, of course. That's what the boys did, most reliably. But in the city below, there was now some new presence, some new mystery. A new potential partner with whom

Catherine saw that her own purposes and potential might be most compellingly aligned. No friend of hers. Her enemy instead. Not Morris, but Kate Speir. She had closed the distance, after all. And she would see the symmetries. Catherine made better sense as a partner than Morris, every time. Hadn't Valerie seen that immediately? And Speir would get it too, when they were face to face. When the gaze met the gaze.

With that conviction, she descended from the mountain, plummeting fast. And when she strode into DIY, it was with a different sense of things. She returned energized and committed despite the threat. First time in a long time, she felt truly unbreakable. Her pod of desks. Her bright blue plastic chairs. Her chattering bro-coders, Metallica soundtrack, poster art, whiteboard hieroglyphs, line of deer antlers along one wall and sparrows in the rafters, yes indeed.

Friday night, 8:00 p.m., Catherine at her workstation, coming up for breath. And though there was by that point hardly a sound in the place but for traffic noise trickling in from Terminal Avenue, she saw she was not alone. One other person was still there at that late hour. Someone with a task list and items outstanding. Someone doing this because they liked it enough to do it well. And it cheered her further to see that the remaining person, late on a Friday, was Kalmar.

"Hey," she called.

He came over. "Haven't seen you around, Red."

"Busy, busy," she told him.

"You look tired," Kalmar said.

"No doubt. I'm beat."

"Idea," he said. "Go home."

"Yeah, right," she said.

"I'm serious," he said. "What exactly is there to do at this hour?"

"I've got a few things here."

He stepped closer to her desk, tattooed hand brushing the top of her monitor. Blue torn sweater, black jeans, boots. Wool cap, check.

Kalmar whose mother surely must have been a staggering beauty. "Well, I got a few more things too," he said now. "And I'm still heading out."

But he didn't. He lingered. And Catherine didn't mind, entirely. He did have that quality. You didn't mind him close. Smelling his wool sweater and the faint aroma of shampoo. Lilac.

He was looking at his fingernails, immaculate. He said it finally: "So are the rumours true, or false, or possibly not for comment?"

She nodded. Okay. So obviously Kalmar would know. And as markets director, he might have wished to be told further out than a week before the deadline. "Who told you?"

He shrugged. He'd rather not say.

"I was going to talk to you all about it eventually."

"That's good," he said, dark eyes up now and on her own.

"The rumours are true. The likely outcome is unclear."

"Buy-sell?"

She sighed. "That's right."

"You just gotta swing that financing, I guess," he said. "How'd it go with the bankers the other day?"

"Bankers are weasels," Catherine said. "Never there when you need them."

Kalmar nodded grimly. "Truth," he said. "Go private. I know people."

"Thanks, Kali," she said. "I know you do, but I'll figure it out."

"Well, if you don't," he said. And here he fell to silence, either unsure quite how to say what came next, or perhaps unsure if it should be said. "If you end up taking the offer and leaving, whatever you're doing next, if you can see a role for me I'd be interested. I like this."

He made a gesture with his finger, back and forth between them. And Catherine, who had thought to stand right then, come around the desk and give him a friend hug of thanks, did not do that now. She just stayed seated and nodded.

"Thanks again," she said. "But don't plan on it. I'm not going anywhere."

"Good to hear," he said. "Good to hear."

"Sorry, Kali, I cut you off the other day. In the car."

Oh that. He glanced up, remembering. Someone had visited the Warehouse that afternoon. Didn't ask for her. Didn't ask for anyone. Just walked in and started to look around. Like an inspection or something. A woman, late thirties maybe.

Catherine sat straighter in her chair. Kalmar only chuckled and shook his head with a confused expression.

"Okay what?" she asked him. "Kalmar, talk to me. What happened?"

"Nothing. No, no. It's just weird. This one thing."

"Tell me, please."

Just this one funny thing, Kalmar said. And here he held his hands up as if to frame a picture of her face: her hair and eyes, the spray of freckles across her nose. "I'm not talking identical twin stuff or anything. But this lady looked quite a lot like you."

MAKO EQUITY LLC

"HI, IT'S ME. VAL, LISTEN. Okay, honestly I'm maybe just a bit freaking out here. Tell me please that you went down to DIY a couple days back and didn't tell them you were my sister. I need to hear from you. I left a message on your other phone. Sorry. Okay, bye."

It was after midnight. She was calling her sister's cell, which was probably turned off and charging, sitting next to her on a bedside table while she peacefully slept, Mark spooned in behind her.

Settle down. Settle down. Have some wine. More wine, that is. No, don't. Shit. It's after midnight. When did I become a person who's up after midnight surrounded by my only friends and they're all in bottles? Pinot grigio BFF. Xanax, Klonopin, Paxipam, Valium, Ativan. I love you guys.

She didn't take anything. She poured her half glass of wine down the sink. She was too agitated, too nervy to drink. Freaking out and not going to deny it.

You said you had something for me?

Catherine looked long and hard at the text she'd written to Rostock, thumb hovering over Send. Quivering there. Trembling. Then over to Delete. Gone. No way.

She was out on the street, in front of her building. At some point in the past half hour she'd exited her own apartment, descended via elevator or stairs, left the building and walked across to the park. She couldn't remember a bit of it. She just seemed to wake up there, sitting on a bench in her robe and slippers.

"What's happening to me?" she said aloud. "What exactly is going on?"

Her face in her hands, eyes pinched shut. Familiar feelings now. G-forces seeming to press her from all sides, compress her. Gravity threatening to do its work. Black shapes thudding around her, pressing close, feathers and beaks and claws. The sensation of falling.

Catherine on a bench in Kitsilano Park. Catherine being approached by a stranger, open hands in front of him, dishevelled, possibly drunk. "Are you okay? Do you need me to call anyone?"

"I'm freaking out in public," she said to the stranger. "Wearing a bathrobe."

"Are you hurt? Do you need help getting home?"

"I'm talking to a stranger in the park across from my apartment in the middle of the night."

"I'm just going to help you cross the street, all right?"

She was safely escorted back across the street and dropped at her front door where she realized she'd locked herself out and had to retrieve spare keys from the back of the building where she'd hidden them behind a hydro meter box. She knocked over a recycling bin. Someone yelled from across the way. She fell asleep at 3:30 a.m. Woke up curled into a fetal ball on the couch. Woke to her phone ringing. It was Val.

"Oh God," Catherine said. "What time is it?"

"So do I worry about you leaving me weird messages in the middle of the night sounding honestly like maybe alcohol was involved?" That was Val at her sharply caring best. They had mothered each other for a long time now. No changing that pattern.

"Ugh," Catherine said. "Tell me now. Were you there?"

Val hadn't been down to DIY, no. She'd never been down. "I don't even know where it is, Cate."

Catherine told her sister about the visitor. Kalmar's comment.

She heard Val breathing evenly at the other end. "Cate," her sister said, "that is nothing to panic about."

Catherine got off the couch and shuffled to the front window. The sky was laced with pink again, dark clouds in the east. She looked across the water to those buildings facing her from the far side of the bay. Kensington Place seemed to glow in special sharpness, butter-yellow accents winking across the waves. The light of the morning sky was reflected there and held her eye.

"Phil told me Mako has moved to Vancouver," Catherine told her sister. "That means Speir is here. You can see why I'm wondering."

"Like what, now Kate Speir looks like you?"

"I don't know," Catherine said. "Who else would just drop by?"

"Who else?" Valerie said. "It could be anybody. Listen. Has your intern found their office address yet?"

No, Arwen hadn't come up with anything. But Valerie wasn't deterred.

"We'll find it. I'm good at finding things. Then you go talk to them. It's just business, right?"

"Right," Catherine said. "Just business."

"It is!" Val said.

"If you say so."

"Come on," her sister said. "Rule of Stephens."

Catherine let out a big breath. Sure, of course. Listen to sister Val. "Didn't you used to go to fortune tellers?" she asked.

"Hey, sometimes they were scary accurate," Valerie said. "But listen. You sit tight. Or better, go to work and get busy with something. Do not fret. And no caffeine, alcohol or red meat today."

Catherine stood at the window, looking out over the park, the buildings on the far side. The sea. Boats and birds. Black birds in their dozens in the trees across the street. They would start up in a swirl, then resettle, as if the wind itself were tossing them, bits of paper or soot.

"So Rostock," Catherine said. "He texted me yesterday. I ignored it."

Valerie took a few seconds to respond. Then she said, "That's probably best, really. For you, I mean."

"Yeah, but then I tried to text him back last night."

"Oh Catherine," Valerie said.

"No answer, so I went looking online. He's completely disappeared. You remember when he called and I Googled him? Got that one hit?"

University of Chicago, Professor Emeritus.

"The page is down," Catherine said. And there was nothing else out there. No address. She'd tried texting but got no answer.

"Where are you going with this?" Valerie asked.

Catherine sighed. She didn't know. Her mind was bouncing between things. "You think DIY has security cameras? I realize I've never even looked."

"Why don't you come over tonight?" Valerie said. "You really don't sound great. Mark will make lasagna. We'll watch *Mamma Mia*. It's Saturday. So we watch Pierce Brosnan sing 'When All Is Said and Done.'"

"I'll try," she said to Val. "I'll really try."

But of course she didn't go. And she didn't follow Val's advice and go to work to stay busy either. She spent the night at home, fretting and watching television without remembering a bit of it. Then she crashed into a pinot-noir-and-Zopiclone-aided sleep at 10:00 p.m., curled up again, same spot, same sofa.

Sunday. Deadline minus six days and counting. Also notable: two hangovers in a row. She really had to get busy with something.

10:38 A.M. *Hi it's Catherine again. Sorry to be a pest.*

11:12 A.M. *I notice your former faculty page is down. Everything all right?*

2:20 P.M. *Well I just called. Message says voice mailbox full. Call me back?*

There were a handful of people in, even though it was Sunday. Catherine heard the ping-pong ball going back and forth. She counted fourteen bikes.

"Go team," she said, rounding the corner and into the space, across to her own workstation. Various voices called back and Catherine had a brief moment of feeling everything was utterly normal. She sat back in her chair, stretched her legs.

She stood up again. "Kali?"

"Not in," someone called back. "Later, I think."

"Do we have video cameras in this place? As in surveillance?" She was looking around now, not seeing anything.

One of the guys from Kali's team came over. He was grinning, pointing up over her head. She craned her neck back and saw the lens nestled into the elbow of one of the roof members. "Huh," she said. "How could I not have noticed that?"

"Live to web," he said. "It's part of our Customer Connect program."

"Seriously," she said. "Is that safe?"

"It's a super-wide picture. Nobody's reading emails over your shoulder."

"Pictures of me, out there?" she said. "I don't know if I love that."

She pulled up the DIY website and clicked through to the Warehouse app. The image opened up. And there she was, hunched over her keys. She could see the programmer too, standing there in front of her desk. "Look at that," she said. "There we are."

"Anything else?" he said.

"Archives?"

"Archive tab maybe?" he said, winking at her.

"Hey," she said, as he walked away. "I saw that." He laughed and didn't turn around.

Back on the site, Catherine clicked through to the archives and found that the site designers were keeping edited clips from previous days. Notable moments, life in DIY. Many of the moments Catherine had no memory of herself. A meeting at one of the pods ending in high-fives. Somebody rolling a vintage Harley-Davidson into the Warehouse, which was immediately surrounded by people. Lots of dog clips, as there were always dogs around. Hapok's Vizsla, Cooper. A Great Dane that belonged to a woman in social media. A snip of film showing people entering the teepee. Someone doing a handstand. It was an odd feeling to think that all of this had happened here while she was sitting in that very desk and unaware. A sign of success, perhaps, that so much life was facilitated. She opened another one, at random: a clip of her walking down the length of the Warehouse. Catherine stared at this one intently, mesmerized. It was from behind, so her face wasn't visible. But it was so clearly her. Slow steps, head down. When had this been taken and what had she been thinking? She looked to be brooding, perplexed. Walking, looking out over the workstations as though assessing the status of things, getting the *sitch* as the boys liked to say. And it was thinking of that word, the *situation*, that brought her sharply to her present one, and the sudden dawning awareness, just as Kalmar entered the bottom of the frame in the video and approached her from behind, that it wasn't her at all.

Not her. And once sensed, it was as if a blindfold had fallen away. She didn't walk like that. She was always in more of a hurry. She wasn't prone to brooding, to pacing around with her hand on her chin. She didn't survey the Warehouse as if she'd never been there before, as though she were doing a head count or sizing up the inventory.

Her heartbeat was up, her skin was flushed, she felt herself sweating lightly, sitting in place. The fight-or-flight response, as if her body was already anticipating action.

This is how adrenalin affected her, Catherine thought. It made her stupid. The smarter person recognized that death was probably not impending despite the adrenal medulla's frantic misfirings, all that catecholamine, norepinephrine, epinephrine storming through the system. You had to suppress it through sheer will or here was a cocktail of neurotransmitters that would turn you into a beast.

Catherine thought she was becoming a beast. She was in her car, driving nowhere. Looking in her rear-view mirror the whole time, wondering if she was being followed. Noticing herself wondering if she was being followed. Worried about wondering what she was wondering. And always at the moment of chasing herself off that line of thinking, seeing a car with darkened windows change lanes at the same time she did, or a van pull out in front of her and drive very slowly, someone's face in the rear-view. That guy was looking at me. I mean, I'm not making this up.

Val called. Score, she said. She had an address for Mako Equity.

"Well that was fast," Catherine managed, thinking only that at the moment this was information she hardly had the strength to use.

A few degrees of separation indeed. Turned out husband Mark knew a lot of angel investors through dealings with his own fund. One of them was Gorman's husband.

"Stephanie Gorman?" Catherine asked.

The same. So Valerie had picked up the phone and called her. Client privilege be damned, just a conversation off the record. "I think she likes you," Val said to Catherine. "She agreed."

Gorman put Valerie and her husband in touch. He actually lived most of the year in Palo Alto, where he was an engineer at Google. But he was also a member of an angel investing co-op called the Kaizen Forum. They got together monthly to look at pitches from start-ups. Members voted and the group threw their money behind projects. One of the investments made a year before was to fund development of a hook-up app for foodies called Salivacious.

"Hook-up app for foodies," Catherine said. "I swear to God I can't tell if you're joking."

Valerie wasn't joking. Nor was Gorman's husband. The user did an initial profile, including a cheek swab to obtain a DNA sample—there was a proprietary disposable swab tool used with the application—and the app created a personal flavour profile. Salty, sweet, sour, spicy, umami, et cetera.

"Like a Myers-Briggs test for foodies who want to have sex, basically. After that it works pretty much like a combo of Tinder and Urbanspoon."

"Wow," Catherine said. "Technology making the world a better place."

"Maybe not," Valerie said. "But Mako bought them."

That was three months ago. The Kaizen group was taken out. And something about the way the deal was negotiated made it clear to Gorman's husband that Mako was in acquisitions mode. They were looking at very particular kinds of software and applications.

"They're building something out of parts," Catherine said. "I get it. I guess DIY has a fit. But I feel like they're pressuring me. These strange things that have been happening."

Valerie was silent for a few seconds. Then she said, "Maybe none of it is really that strange."

"Some of it seems really goddamn strange to me," Catherine said.

"Try not to think that way," Valerie said. "Mako wants DIY. But so do you. So you defend yourself with what you can. Go talk to them. You got a pen?"

Valerie the finder. She'd somehow accomplished this through a friend who was a realtor. That friend got talking to her own network, looking for quick sales to numbered companies. "A realtor's hunch," Valerie explained. "The buyer is really rich and two weeks ago they were based in Seattle. So Mako wasn't shopping for fun."

"And this other realtor just coughed up the info?"

Turns out agents loved to boast among themselves. The woman who gave up the address that cross-referenced to a numbered company owned by Mako Equity and sold the week prior didn't even ask for anything in exchange. It was a status thing, Valerie said.

Valerie was being so level-headed these days. Catherine longed for the luxury. She was in the commercial district of East Vancouver now, just off the waterfront. She pulled over and turned off the engine. There was a woman standing on the opposite corner, cigarette in the corner of her mouth. They made eye contact. The woman looked away, watching for cars.

"I'm pulled over," Catherine told her sister. "I'm parked across the street from a prostitute who looks to have a pretty serious methamphetamine problem. I wonder how her day is going."

Catherine had fished a pen out of her purse and an envelope to write on. She was pretty sure she wouldn't be going over to confront Speir immediately. She'd wait until Monday to steel herself. But she'd get the data, gather what she could to use in her own defence.

She wrote the number down: 1300 block Nicola Street. She folded the envelope and tucked it into her purse. Then they talked about not much for a moment before hanging up.

Catherine sitting in a tiny car in a bad part of town. She saw the woman opposite was gone, but hadn't noticed her getting picked up. And what if she had noticed? What would she have done? She could have written down the licence plate number or followed the car. She could have done a whole range of things and still had no effect on the scene as it played out in front of her, as it played out in that woman's life.

Catherine thought about that, about being essentially powerless. And then, it came to her all at once, in a dark rush. It was as if the windows of the car had suddenly tinted, the light gone blue and textured, blurred. A sound in her ears, too, a sharp ringing, instant, penetrating. Her heart rate was up, and her breathing. Nicola Street was in the West End. Just across the water.

The phone in her hand trembled violently as she punched the address into Maps:1386 Nicola Street.

And there it came. Crucial information she wished she didn't have to process just that second: 1386 Nicola Street was at the corner of Nicola and Beach Avenue. Kate Speir wasn't just in Vancouver. Kate Speir had bought a place staring across False Creek pretty much directly into Catherine's living room window; 1386 Nicola was Kensington Place. And seeing it on the map, the distance between them the width of a fingernail, Catherine's hand began to shake so hard that she dropped the phone and heard it rattle and bounce to a spot directly under her seat.

Catherine and Kate. Cate and Kate. Catherine thought she could feel dominos falling inside her, some process unleashed. Because there was no longer a reasonable explanation for these data points she was plotting, not in Hawking territory anyway. And that meant she was nudging and slouching and sliding on down into that lower and darker land of King.

The beast had stirred powerfully again. She was driving too fast now. She was parking illegally. She was pulling on the big glass front door to Phil's office building, and pulling and continuing to pull for probably three full minutes before she realized that Phil's office wouldn't be open on Sunday and that even Phil tried to take his weekends off.

So she took the highway. Out into West Vancouver. Swerving past cars on Taylor Way, then up the ramp and onto the Upper Levels Highway. She was stopped for speeding about thirty seconds later: $225, and it could have been much worse. They normally impounded the car when people were more than sixty kilometres an hour over the limit, the officer told her. He was staring down through the small window at her, hands on his thighs.

"Have you been crying, miss?" he asked.

No, she had not been crying. Okay, emotional. Yes, she was driving out that very minute to talk to her lawyer, or at least the man who used to be her lawyer, and she'd been thinking about that and not her foot on the gas until she saw the flashing lights and noticed she was going 150 kilometers per hour.

"I honestly didn't think this thing could go that fast," she said. "Totally my fault."

The cop was still crouched in that same position, like he was talking to a child.

"I think I know you from somewhere," the cop said, expression very focused.

Okay, here we go, Catherine thought. It took him a few tries. Did she work on television? Was she in the movies? Then she gave him his answer.

"Air France Flight 801," she said. "Brittas Bay."

"Wow," he said, solemnly. But at least he didn't have any theories. And he didn't tell her how lucky she was, either. He seemed merely to think that she could use a break. And he reached into the car to shake her hand before leaving. Saying thank you and please stay safe.

Please stay safe.

She drove more slowly that last distance to Phil's house, five minutes. Ten, tops. Emotions brimming fresh.

"What's wrong?" Phil said. "Oh geez."

He was hugging her. She was getting a hug from her ex-lawyer. Trying not to sob into his shoulder. They were standing on the front steps of his uselessly large white house with its forest and ocean views and the ghost of his long-gone marriage.

They walked in through the house and sat in the kitchen. Out the porch windows, she could see the sky growing stormy to the west. Up through the chute of the Strait of Georgia, something very big seemed ready to roll in from the sea. The wind was up. And as Phil put the water to boil, Catherine sat with her chin in her hands, eyes out on the horizon, seeing the darkness there, the bruised brown and grey of the clouds, the air heavy with water and heading in their direction fast.

Phil came back with cups of tea. He had a plate of cookies too. "Is this how people do it?" he asked.

Catherine looked up at him.

"Is this how you entertain when someone drops over? I don't know. She used to do all that."

Catherine had met her once. Wide-set eyes, the coils and flows of jet-black hair, glossy and aromatic with floral shampoos. A dancer, she'd been told.

"You're doing fine," she said to Phil. Then gesturing to the cookies, "Yes, please."

Phil sat heavily. He looked more tired than Catherine ever remembered seeing him. His eyes were red and rimmed darkly. His forehead held high and creased, some permanent question outstanding.

"So I'm processing all this, okay," he said, finally. She'd told him the truth about dinner with Rostock. The mad things that had been said. She'd told him told him about Speir in the Warehouse, on the video. What Gorman's husband had added: Mako in acquisitions mode. And more, Speir in Vancouver. Speir in Kensington Place, where Catherine had herself for so long imagined living. She'd gone further too, told Phil about feeling hemmed in and encroached and shadowed.

Then she'd stopped. "I sound hysterical," she'd said. "I fully realize it. I hate myself like this but I can't just pretend these things haven't happened."

Phil's face was directed towards the glass. He appeared to be squinting into the wind that was not reaching him, only making the house quietly groan and creak. She herself felt this wind on her skin like cold blades, her skin hurting, her nerve endings jangling. She sipped her tea then set it down. Hugged herself closely.

"I don't know," Phil said, getting up and walking back into the kitchen. He was at a loss for words, she realized. It was all clearly too crazy for him and he was embarrassed. She decided she wasn't going to cry again. Just don't let that happen. Other people didn't deserve it. But some other variety of frustration and anxiety was rising within her, and Phil could surely read it.

She stood up and went to the window. She looked out at the storm clouds to the west and thought about Saturna Island, the hobby farm there. A peaceful arrangement that under other circumstances she might herself have enjoyed. But Phil wasn't following her gaze. He'd come back across the room, but was looking at her instead, looking at her profile with a wistful, helpless expression on his kind, round face.

Here was a pragmatic man, who wasn't superstitious or weird in any way. A regular guy, approaching his middle years, who wore size 43 suits and twenty-year-old rugby shirts on the weekend. He had hundreds of clients and very few friends. Catherine knew all these things about him from years of observation, and so she also knew now that his mind was working on an explanation and failing to find one, unwilling to contemplate a world where explanations went missing.

Fair enough, Catherine thought. And fair too that she might now have to find these explanations on her own, even if it meant looking in unusual places.

Phil had said nothing in several minutes. But Catherine saw that something had just come to him. She lifted her head and looked at him squarely. He made a gesture that they should step outside. And sliding the glass doors, he went out onto that wide, seaward deck. When they were at the railing together, with the wind swirling around them, he started to speak in a low voice, telling her what he could. And as he spoke, Catherine felt something in her taking a firmer shape. It had a real form and substance. Like a new body growing inside her own, filling her out to the skin.

There had been other Mako Equity acquisitions, Phil confirmed. Valerie could never have found this out. Gorman's husband wouldn't have known. But they knew in house, at Phil's firm.

"I'm into actual lawyerly misconduct here," he said. "But I'd like you to have some context. It might help you see this picture more clearly."

The other purchases were all in the start-up phase as well. And that was notable in itself. Mako was a huge fund. They didn't take positions in start-ups, or never had previously. They bought mining companies. Or airlines. They'd had an interest in private security for a long time, holdings in two of the world's largest military contractors. Then suddenly, a year ago, this new thing. A genetics modeller called Helixer. A back-end massive-scale file architecture management tool called LogJam. A portable medical records database called MedRec. Salivacious she knew about already, in essence a DNA collection and matching technology.

If Morris was now teamed up with people building something out of those particular parts, Phil was saying, well then Catherine probably wanted to take a step back and think about that.

"DNA analysis. Database architecture. Genetic manipulation code. Add to that a diagnostic ingestible. And all that plugging into an infrastructure with deep ties to the global security sector. That all suggests to me a bigger picture I don't even want to see. But if you're targeted by an entity of that kind," Phil said, pausing. "I'm going to tell you as a friend, as a person who cares about you, let it go. Let Morris win. I don't know the reasons why this is the right choice for you. I just know that it is."

Catherine's brain was ringing now. Multiple streams of information ticker-taping through. Video and audio tracks, none of them properly synched. Speir in the Warehouse. Kalmar under those looming sculptures, gesturing towards the invasive species that would either displace her, or that she would have to become herself. And a beat track, a beat track that would not go away. *Confront and defeat. Confront and defeat.*

Morris in his boardroom with his Western art and his Apple watch, silver hair, plans and more plans in which she was supposed to co-operate by being some tiny spinning cog, aligned and coordinated with his great and invisible purpose. Morris on his biggest payday of all.

She'd been agitated and nervous, she'd been afraid. All of these emotions seemed to have been flushed through her, forced by pressure from the outside, a pressure driven by the mounting suspicion that natural law had gone awry, that something had soured in the world such that rules were being broken and hidden things were entering the real by doorways that had always previously been closed. Agitation, nerves and fear. Those had been the right feelings for the moments of escalating doubt in which they occurred. But those moments were past. The right feeling for that moment, having just heard what Phil had to tell her, was the angry will to truth. She had to resolve herself and face it. Hawking or King. A lifetime certainty now hung in the balance. And it was time to know.

"How long do I have?" she asked Phil.

He lifted his head, looked at her. He was surprised at the question. Surely even if he weren't acting for her legally and there to constantly remind her, she could remember the day count that late in the game. But he told her. It was Sunday. The deal closed Friday one way or the other.

"Why?" he asked her, a trace of nervousness in his voice.

The new body inside her had expanded to fill her completely. She could feel it, taut under her skin. A new entity indeed. A new Catherine Bach. And that new Catherine Bach was angry.

Morris, she thought. Dr. Rostock. Let's try this one more time.

SHE FLEW.

No alcohol. No prescription meds, though she went back and forth on those. Catherine in the bathroom, getting things together in a hurry, Paxipam in hand, face in the mirror looking sober and strong. She thought about it. Then she thought about tossing the bottle into the trash. Then, immediately: *Let's be serious.*

She packed that and some Zopiclone for sleeping. And the Ativan.

Then the thought came again, much more forcefully.

"Be serious," she said, aloud this time. And she took the time to look at that face in the mirror, consider the story of how that face came to be there, regarding itself with new seriousness, new resolve. And she took those pills out of her kit and did exactly what she had seconds before known that she must do. She dropped the bottles one by one into the trash, death rattle after death rattle. She felt free.

Clothes into a carry-on open on the bed. A flannel shirt and a wool sweater, jeans and socks and athletic underwear. A fleece because it would be cold. Black gloves and a scarf. No heels required. Catherine watched herself pack. She was grateful to see the return of this more instinctual person. This woman of direction, if not yet certainty. That would follow. It had to.

Valerie called when the airport taxi was on the way. Catherine hadn't told her about the trip and felt momentarily guilty. But her sister wasn't calling to check up on her. Turn on CNN, Valerie said.

An expert talking about AF801, second anniversary approaching. They were going to talk about lightning. They were going to mention the fifth man theories and the misfiring Russian space-based laser. They were going to speculate about bird strikes this time around.

"No matter that we were at 28,000 feet," Catherine said, sitting in her living room, watching the television with her sister on the line.

"Birds don't fly that high?"

"An Andean condor maybe," Catherine said. "A bar-headed goose over the Himalayas. Not that I checked or anything."

"What about the whooper swan?" Valerie asked. "They just mentioned that one. Here's a species been seen up to 27,000 feet over Northern Ireland."

"It wasn't a whooper swan," Catherine said. "I was there."

"Okay, forget it," Valerie said. Then, "You sound different. Are you going somewhere?"

Chicago, she said. And she was right to anticipate Valerie's response. Didn't she think all that was best left alone? Did she even have time for this now?

Catherine's eyes drifted to the window. False Creek. A tiny smudge of yellow on the far shore. She tore her eyes off the view. "I have to know," she said. "I can't let all this happen without understanding what it means."

Valerie was far from convinced. "Rushing off. Not thinking," she said. "This is really out of character for you."

"It is," Catherine said. "I don't deny it."

"So you go confront Morris?"

It was partly that. Certain things had to be said. The man had quite possibly been messing with her.

"And Dr. Rostock?" Valerie said, emotion rising. "A man you were convinced had a brain injury? A man who might be dangerous?"

A man who had something for her. But Catherine didn't tell her sister that. Her comments were all valid, only Valerie had not fallen from the sky in such a way that explanations were now finally required.

They didn't argue much. And the arguments had a way of burning out as one or the other of them blew a sisterly breath over the flickering flame. Catherine did that now. She said to Valerie, "Do you remember our angel?"

It took her a second, but Valerie remembered. Up on the mountain, she said. An outline of a wing and a shoulder, an angel in repose, two little feet sticking up.

"I couldn't see it for the longest time," Catherine said to her. "You showed me and I pretended to see it. I never told you that."

Valerie was silent now.

"I wanted to believe that you saw something," Catherine said. "And eventually I understood that you had all along."

Catherine was in the taxi now. Catherine was on her way. That was her shooting out Grant McConachie Way in Richmond, rolling up to departures. That was her breezing through the automatic doors. There she was with a real, printed ticket and a boarding pass. And that was her closing her eyes at takeoff, feeling the surge, the impossible power, that hovering moment of separation.

But not separation. They were in the air. The ground was dropping beneath them. But she was all in herself and still very much herself. And when she blinked and woke, she realized she'd slept through their entire ascent. The seatbelt signs were off. The cabin was darkened, a granular blue. They were at the top of that long vault from which she had herself once so spectacularly fallen. And she was whole.

Out the window the world was black and endless, spreading and entire. And she was very much still in herself as passengers made themselves comfortable in the seats around her, as the body of the plane shuddered around them, very much in one piece as the sound and the pressure enveloped her and held her tight.

—

She took the Blue Line train in, got herself checked in at her hotel in River North, high view of towers in the Loop, the Hard Rock Café, the La Salle Street Bridge. It was Christmas in the city and there were decorations in the windows of stores and wreaths along the bridge railings. Catherine arrived in the morning, having slept on the plane, feeling energized and focused and unbeatable. She walked to Morris's office in the grey light, the sky close, the wind swirling around her.

"Tell him it's Catherine Bach," she said to the receptionist, who'd just told her that Morris was out.

"I'm sorry, Ms. Bach, but—"

"Please tell him it's me," Catherine said. "I've flown in from Vancouver. Please tell him I flew."

"But I'm afraid that won't change the fact that he's . . ."

Catherine sat in the leather chair next to a towering fern and a wide painting of bison grazing the Montana flatlands. Morris, Morris. Who have you been trying to impress?

The receptionist did go away, dutifully. And she did return. She started to speak. Catherine could see her raise a hand, to gesture uselessly. But Catherine didn't lift her head from the copy of *The Economist* she was pretending to read, cover story on conflict in the Middle East. Men standing under pocked concrete arches, Kalashnikovs dangling, stances wide. Don't talk to me, Catherine was thinking, eyes on the page. Let the man show himself. Let him get out of his comfortable chair and walk down that hallway and deal with the entity into which Catherine had transformed.

"You're the client," Stephanie Gorman had said. "But are you sure about this?"

"Write the letter, yes, please," Catherine had told her.

Was this a tenuous plan? Gorman didn't say so. Or she didn't say so again, having said it already at their first meeting. It was going to be a percentage game, threatening in writing to sue Morris. And going to see him was in any case unwise. It would be better to let Gorman do the communicating, but Catherine was not to be stopped.

"I'd like to hand it to him," she told Gorman. "Call it personal satisfaction."

But there was something else in play. Morris had toned down the rhetoric since word of the *Red Pill 2.0* test. He'd gone quiet, and Catherine wondered why.

The receptionist was now looking across the room at her. Catherine smiled and returned to her magazine just as the elevator dinged its arrival in the lobby outside those doors, and out of the corner of her eye, she could see Morris striding towards the glass.

He'd come from somewhere. He'd been doing something else. They'd no doubt called him to say that she was waiting here. And Morris had come back straight away to see her. He did indeed have something of a new air about him. Although it wasn't a quiet feeling exactly. Morris seemed instead to have settled on some course of action that he hadn't felt it necessary to share. And as he made his way down the corridor ahead of her to the boardroom, asking her if she wanted something to drink, commenting on how good she looked, Catherine reflected on how ably Morris put her off balance. Always a degree more certain than her. Always seeming to know one move farther than her into the future. It was unsettling. It was also annoying.

Chai arrived. A carafe of water. A plate of Turkish delight, amber cubes dusted with sugar. She didn't take one. Catherine extracted the letter instead and slid it across the table towards him.

No wavering of Morris's even mood. He took the letter with slightly pursed lips. His brow creased in curiosity. But he did not open it because she'd effectively told him the contents already, by showing up, by the things she had by that point already said. He only set the letter to one side, neatly aligning the long edge with the edge of the table. He squared it away and listened to all that she had to say, which was steadily delivered. And when she was done he sat back in his chair, which creaked with his weight. He coughed into a closed fist.

He said, "Well, this comes as a surprise, certainly. And I can't say I blame you."

Catherine waited. She felt a creeping wariness.

"You built the company," he said. "You want to defend it. I get that."

Out over his shoulder that familiar tableau, helicopters and birds, geysers of steam and turning ventilator fans. Men on distant rooftops in the icy cold. The city ticked and whirred. It generated its very specific sounds and smells, its frictions and pivotal moments.

Then Morris said, "Only, Catherine, I'm no longer the right person to sue."

Mako Equity had bought him out. DIY was a great business, he said. He still believed in it. "Don't get me wrong on that. But they named an irresistible price."

Catherine was confused. They knew all this already, didn't they?

No, Morris said, leaning forward now for emphasis. No, she didn't. Or she wasn't understanding the crucial issue. Morris's share in DIY was held by Parmer Ventures. "And that's what they just bought," he said. And here he made a gesture with his hands as if dusting off his palms. *No muss, no fuss. I'm out.*

Mako bought Parmer Ventures, the whole fund and all of its assets. And since the shotgun offer originated from Parmer Ventures, Mako now owned that too.

"You want to sue someone to stop this thing," Morris had said to her, "go take a run at Mako. And good luck."

And here he slid the envelope Catherine had just given him back across the table towards her.

—

Catherine was back at her hotel, sky over the lake gone deep blue. Colours up along the avenues. Michigan Avenue was magical with its thousands of winking lights. She'd walked a long time after the meeting, heavy sweater, wool scarf, gloves. Down and along the river, then into the Christkindlmarket in Daley Plaza where there was a brass band playing oompah music and stalls selling trinkets and tree ornaments, the smell of pretzels and mustard in the air. She wondered if Rostock and his wife had come here back in their day. She wondered if this was the kind of homey thing that they might have enjoyed during the years before the trauma and the changes. That slow wrong turning.

She'd followed the crowds and ended up in a shop devoted to German glass Christmas ornaments, a bewildering variety in gaudy colours. A section devoted to barn animals and another to dogs. Birds, insects. Sailboats, mushrooms and Disney figures. There were glass ornaments in the shapes of famous structures and build-ings, the Washington Monument, the Eiffel Tower, the World Trade Center. She thought about that one, turning the blue frosted glass piece over in her hands, considering whether it was in the poorest of taste or if she perhaps did not remember any longer how ordinary people processed grief by remembering the good. Wasn't it a mental artifact of the greatest possible good, even seasonal joy, to see those slender towers in their glassy original state, new and unblemished? And this was a drifting line of thinking that she might have followed further had her eye not tracked ahead across the long shelf of baskets, each with its own ornament, and found the section devoted to airplanes.

A Concorde. A 747.

An Airbus A380-800 in Air France livery.

She held the fragile object between trembling fingers. She thought to drop it, to let it smash to the floor. That would in some way be the truthful thing to do. But she set it down gently instead, nestled it among the many duplicates in that basket, each one pristinely whole and living in the lie of what had been before and could not be regained.

Now she was back in the hotel sipping a glass of pinot noir, staring out to the darkening eastern horizon, a familiar black lake. She thought to phone Valerie, but decided against it. It felt right to go this one alone. Morris was out. That forced her to measure the situation in a different way. After all that posturing and threatening and visiting the Warehouse and strutting around like he was taking charge, high-fiving the bros and generally making an ass of himself, he was now playing the fact that he no longer had an interest in DIY as though that had been his plan all along.

Go take a run at Mako. And good luck.

Catherine looked out the hotel window and saw the city there, a smear of lights and a suggestion of shapes. She'd figure it out. She'd know what to do. Perhaps as soon as tomorrow. As soon as she'd seen Dr. Rostock, perhaps all would then be clear. The truth of their connection. The truth of who they both really were.

Rostock's apartment was on South Drexel in Hyde Park. The address had come by text just after she'd left Phil's house that past Sunday. She'd sat in the car and messaged him. *I've booked a flight. I'm coming back to Chicago.*

And before she could pocket the phone, the return text came in. *We should speak by phone.*

I'm coming. I need to see you.

Minutes passed. She did not move. Then it came. Address only. *Message when you arrive.* She responded herself, right away. *Tuesday AM. Will msg.* But there was no further reply.

Rostock's suite number suggested he was on the top floor. And on the sidewalk out front she let her eyes drift up to find the row of leaded-glass windows there that swept the front of the suite. To the right, a turret, where she imagined him sitting and reading, or writing, or doing whatever it was that now occupied him.

There was an aluminum box next to a locked gate with apartment numbers and call codes. Catherine pressed the one for Rostock's suite and heard the faint purr of the buzzer. Once, twice, three times. Then voicemail, though not Rostock's voice. A woman. *We're out. Please leave a message.*

It surprised her. She'd texted from the airport and given the time of her expected arrival in Hyde Park. After all his earlier efforts to reach her, she'd assumed he'd be here. Plus, Rostock hadn't mentioned he lived with anyone, although it had been ten years since his wife died, assuming that whole story was true.

Cars were singing down the boulevard. The wind was up and the bare trees were rattling their branches overhead. It occurred to Catherine that she wasn't getting anything done just standing there. That she did have a clock ticking, however wearily limited her ability to affect the outcome seemed now to be. Her flight left that same afternoon. She had to do something.

So she texted again. And this time she didn't entirely hide the irritation she was feeling. She was in the city. She'd come all that way. And there she was standing in the chill on South Drexel outside his apartment. Did he think he might have a moment to reply?

It took five minutes before it came in. And when it did—she had her phone set to buzz twice for text notifications, a fuzzed-up heartbeat, an arrhythmic stutter step—she had just decided to head south on the boulevard, not knowing where she was going exactly, just knowing she had to head somewhere. The phone did its hiccup buzz and she started as it seemed to jump slightly in her gloved hand.

Can you wait 10 minutes? I'll be right over.

She was in her mid-fifties and had serious eyes. Dr. Helena Lee. She arrived by taxi, climbed out pulling a quilted jacket tightly around her. Catherine could see a white lab coat underneath. Hard to read the mood. The woman's was stern, and her handshake was firm to the point of being a challenge. She let them in the high black gate and led Catherine up the walk.

"You were expecting Michael," Dr. Lee said, just as they reached the door. Hand on the doorknob, key in hand. She didn't turn around. "I have his phone. Let's get in out of this cold."

They climbed the stairs, footfalls dampened on thick carpet, the flights narrowing as they rose. Up and up. And then they were inside. Golden hardwood floors. A long dining room table by the front windows that she had looked up at earlier from the sidewalk below. There was a shelf of books and a trolley with wine and liquor bottles. There was an area rug across the centre of the room and various comfortably overstuffed chairs. Through a door to the left, Catherine could see the turret room where she had imagined Rostock reading, heavy oak desk with a leather top.

"Dr. Lee . . ." Catherine began.

"Helena, please," she said. She was making tea and gestured that Catherine should sit.

Lee returned from the kitchen with milk and sugar. She addressed her own cup with a focused expression. Then she lifted her face to look at Catherine squarely. She was sorry that Catherine had come all this way. And she thought she understood why Catherine and Michael had been in touch.

"You'd been through something so horrible," Lee said. "I can only imagine that you would have found support and understanding in one another."

A sensation was sweeping her, one that she had not felt in several days but which was now rapidly onrushing.

Of course. Of course. And Catherine heard her voice at a whisper. *Of course*. Because there had never been a reason to ask. She knew.

Michael Rostock had committed suicide the week prior. And here

Dr. Lee's tears flowed and she looked away. Catherine caught movement at the periphery of her vision. A watching other. An awakening. An awareness of the world again altering its shape such that nothing would look the same after she and Dr. Lee had finished speaking.

They'd been romantically involved. Lee's words, carefully chosen. Rostock's wife had been gone many years. He was trying to move on, to be healthy in all ways. He'd gone to Paris to his conference. Lee and Rostock had planned to be married on his return. It would have been a very quiet ceremony. Just a few friends. Some colleagues from the hospital.

"But he had a difficult time after the accident." Lee paused, straightening and collecting herself. "His physical injuries weren't severe. But he came home broken in other ways."

It wasn't obvious at first, but then more and more. He couldn't sleep. He was agitated and nervous. He startled easily. You couldn't approach him from behind. He began to shut himself in. He stopped going to work.

"This created enormous pressure at the hospital," Lee said. "You have to understand. Everyone loved him. He was respected. But when he stopped showing up daily, things began to fall apart."

Rostock had trials on the go that required supervision. He'd delayed several of them, obsessed with minor data anomalies. These had grown more complicated and perplexing. Senior staff had grown resentful at his absences and frictions had arisen. Eventually there were those on the team who thought the entire data set had been corrupted.

"The hospital asked me to talk to him," Lee said. "They had real questions. But by that point he'd pushed me completely away. It was like I was living with a ghost. Eventually Michael took another apartment, as if he were abandoning his entire life."

His identity had been stolen, he told her. He thought he was being followed, that the person in question was responsible for problems at work, that this person was in fact his double, spawned somehow by the accident. He spoke of doppelgängers.

Doppelgänger. Ankou. Fylgia. Fetch.

He told Lee that he was tracking down other AF801 survivors, to warn them. That he'd identified some kind of symmetry that existed among the six of them.

"I never thought that was a healthy thing for him to do. I'm sorry but I didn't."

"It actually meant a great deal to me," Catherine said.

Well, it seemed only to make Rostock more paranoid and delusional, Lee said. "I tried to get him professional help. He would never agree. I heard from his cousin eventually, who is with the FBI. Michael had gone to them. They were concerned about some of the things he'd been saying. His cousin wanted to know if he was all right."

Lee no longer knew if Rostock was all right. She knew he'd rented a place in Bridgeport, but had never been told exactly where. He said he had to keep this secret because he had his double under observation. He told her that the hospital had asked him to resign.

"Then, one day he contacted me and he sounded quite different."

They met for coffee, and Lee remembered thinking Rostock seemed like he had in some ways returned to normal. He had some of his old poise back. His old confidence. But what he actually told her frightened her even more, convincing her that something was still very wrong. He told her that he had a plan to meet his double.

"'Confront and defeat,' he told me," Lee said. "He kept saying that. I didn't have any idea what he meant. He didn't appear angry. And yet I could sense a kind of rage in him."

"When was this?" Catherine asked.

A few weeks ago, Lee said, which Catherine understood to place the meeting just after Catherine herself had met with Rostock over dinner. But she said nothing about that. Perhaps better not to complicate the memories. Perhaps better for Catherine herself not to over-think the timing relative to his death, those many desperate texts that went unanswered.

"He wasn't doing well, I could see that." Lee paused, wiping her eyes. "But then he was suddenly doing a great deal worse."

Further data anomalies at the lab. Further quiet questions asked. Rostock spiralled off into paranoia again. He disappeared into Bridgeport and was dead a couple of weeks later.

"May I ask how?" Catherine's hand was over her mouth, as if she had not wanted the question to come out.

Toxicology said sleeping pills, Lee told Catherine. But then she paused and Catherine sensed her reservations. She leaned forward and put a hand on Lee's arm, who looked up at her, the tears again brimming.

Lee held a napkin in trembling hands and described the details of Rostock's death that she feared she would never be able to explain. Rostock's landlord had contacted her with the news. She'd gone over to Bridgeport and seen the circumstances to which Rostock had by then been reduced. The place had been utterly destroyed. His furniture and effects. It appeared as if there had been a fight. Neighbours had heard something. The police had attended. It was beyond comprehension.

"A fight with whom?" Catherine asked, aware that she was flushing, her pulse starting to race.

Lee paused to wipe her eyes. "No one," she said. "Or himself. Or someone. I don't know."

Not this, Catherine thought. Please not this.

"He left a note," she said. "I've since destroyed it. Utter madness. He wrote about black birds that surrounded him, that burst out of his chest. He spoke of a fire that consumed him, of beating this doppelgänger to death with his fists."

Catherine sat frozen, listening. Lee breathed deeply for a few seconds.

"The hospital wants it kept very quiet. I want privacy myself. Too much has happened and there is no happy version of the story."

Catherine was sitting back by this point, horrified and riveted. The deathly familiarity of the story. Nancy Whittle. Adrian Janic, Patricia Langston, Douglas Marshall. Dr. Michael Rostock.

Lee was weeping again now, tears streaming down her face. Catherine moved across to sit next to her on the couch, and the older woman leaned into her and let herself be held. Catherine thought she could smell the hospital in her hair, a working doctor in love with another. She imagined they'd met there, at the clinic, in the lab. Eye contact. A shiver of interest. A slow first date. There had been real love here, Catherine thought, as Lee's shoulders shook under the light pressure of her embrace.

"I'm sorry," Lee said, straightening.

Catherine's eyes were on the window. No impulse to tears, but a pressing thought instead. Was she truly the last?

"May I ask a question?" she said, picking up her tea in a steady hand, sipping, waiting.

She had a taxi wait at the end of the block with instructions that she needed fifteen minutes tops and then they had to race to O'Hare. "Flight at 4:30 p.m., we can do this?"

The cabby was a Somalian. He'd told her already he'd been in Mogadishu when the Black Hawks went down. "I'm not boasting," he said. Impeccable accent-free American English. "I was five years old. Yes, we can make it."

She made her way down the block. The streets were empty except for parked cars.

"Did you see his body?" she had asked Dr. Lee at the very end of their conversation. Tea in hand and a sense of impending closure.

It was an odd question, to which Lee had reacted with a startled glance. Yes, she had. Of course she had. Why did Catherine want to know?

"This will sound strange and I apologize in advance. But I believe it's important."

Lee was listening, though her glance flickered briefly over Catherine's shoulder and towards the door.

"Were you certain it was him?"

Catherine moved into the street now, a quick glance up and down. No traffic. An odd stillness over that part of the city. Very little noise but for the scrape of a plane passing overhead, a white seam opening in the dusty blue as if the sky itself were being minutely torn.

Lee had gone stiff with the question. And Catherine sensed that their time together had drawn to a close. "You may not know this," Catherine said, "but I'm also a physician. And I ask for a specific reason."

Well, in that case. Lee drew herself straight in the chair, addressing Catherine squarely. In that case, *Dr. Bach*. And here she'd given Catherine the straight goods. Choroid fissure. *Coloboma*, from the Greek word for *defect*.

"An aperture in the iris," Lee had told Catherine. "If there were such a thing as a *double*, then his was a perfect one. Flaws and all."

Of course it would be, Catherine thought. Faithfulness to the smallest flaw would be the *doppelgänger*'s signal perfection.

And with that, Lee had begged her leave, citing workload, patients. The ordinary madness. And Catherine found herself on South Drexel Boulevard again with a single task left in Chicago.

FINGER OF GOD

CATHERINE DIDN'T EXACTLY HAVE A GAME PLAN. She wasn't sure she even had clear objectives. But she knew the next few necessary steps.

It would be so good to speak. I have something for you.

She knocked on the door at the address on South Halsted that Lee had reluctantly given her. A stocky African-American man in jeans and a Chicago Bulls jersey opened the door. Rostock's landlord. The spark of recognition between them was not commented on. But from the man's expression and the sudden stillness within her, Catherine thought they both seemed to be meeting exactly the person expected.

"My name is Catherine Bach. I think you might have something for me."

She provided identification—a Canadian passport, scrutinized closely—and only then did he pull open the door wide enough for her to enter, beckoning with his free hand that she should come inside.

"I'm sorry about what happened," he said.

Gabriel was his name. He'd had a hard week, Catherine guessed. And as he led her back through the house, he warily answered her first tentative questions. No, he'd never met Dr. Rostock before he rented the ramshackle house two months prior. And no, he hadn't seen him around much since then, as Rostock seemed to come and go at unusual hours. Then Gabriel wondered aloud at how long Rostock's body might have lain in his bedroom, had it not been for the earlier noise complaints.

Catherine asked about that as they made their way past a small kitchen and into a long, dark hall that led to the rear of the main floor.

"Some kind of crazy fight, smashing, yelling, bad language. He did a lot of damage as you'll see. I'm only now starting the cleanup."

"You mean he wasn't alone?"

"Cops came," the landlord said. "Said he was alone, being noisy, but no crime yet. So they left and then this happened. I don't know what to think."

They'd reached the bedroom. And those last words unspooled just as the door swung open and the room came into view. Catherine, both hands to her mouth, in shock. "Oh my God."

The wreckage lay in mounds and dunes and drifts, as if the contents of the entire apartment had been dragged into that back room and put through a wood-chipper. A shelf, its books disgorged, then minutely chopped to ribbons. A couch that existed only as a vague structural reference to its original form and function: confettied upholstery, splintered timbers. A midden of smashed dishes and crockery. Clothes torn and strewn. Evidence of an office turned upside down and shaken: torn sticky notes, mangled bull clips, mulched financial papers, the remnants of many plastic cards. Catherine took a single step into the room, overwhelmed at the completeness of the destruction. She'd seen pictures of tornados that had traced similar patterns on the ground. *Finger of God,* people said, referring to how the created world could be entirely erased. And here too the physical had been stripped out of itself, objects defuncted and depurposed in a single savage swirling. Catherine thought she saw it quite clearly, the tornado of converging convictions that had emerged from Rostock and caused him to lay waste to the very surfaces and substances of his life.

When she returned sufficiently to the moment, to herself standing where she was standing, having swept on through memories of their dinner together, the spiralling agony of the story he told, such anguish at the end in the black depths of his angular *coloboma*, Catherine found her cheeks wet with tears. Finally, finally. Here they came in earnest. And she wrapped her arms around herself and let the sobs wrack her silently for several moments. 70F, she thought, I resisted you but I do believe. I believe you now all too terribly well.

It was a lumpy envelope with her name written across it. But she didn't open it, standing in the wreckage of what Dr. Michael Rostock's life had become. Standing precisely where that life, the penultimate one of those marked, original six, had completed its final disintegration. She didn't think Rostock would have expected her to open it there. Perhaps he'd even forgotten he'd left her anything at all in that maelstrom moment when he wrote his own ending.

She didn't open it in the taxi to O'Hare, or on the plane, either. She just held it in her lap, feeling the shape of several objects inside, until she fell asleep and stayed asleep almost the entire way.

At home, instead. In her living room, on her return. Toby back from the cat sitter's and coiling around her bare ankles. A cup of tea at hand. Her clothes were unpacked and in the washing machine. She had checked email and voicemail but made no replies. One-word email from Kalmar: *Sparrow.*

Next steps. Small but critical next steps.

She sat herself down at the dining room table, slit the envelope open. There were three items, which she extracted one by one. Coordinates of a kind. Plot points for locating oneself in a three-dimensional space.

A man's wristwatch stopped at the fated moment of 10:30 in the evening, the thick crystal smashed in the pattern of a snowflake. Blue diver's bezel. Rostock's watch, frozen forever in the lingering moment of impact, radical and entire.

A folded Air Safety Card from an Air France Airbus A380-800. Catherine noted the picture of the aircraft in the waves with slides extended. The water birth where it all began.

Last item, a small envelope tucked into the larger one. It wasn't sealed and she opened the flap with her finger to see there were photographs inside. Six of them, small headshots swiped off the Internet and printed on ordinary paper. Catherine laid them out on the table. That was Rostock there. And here, a picture of Catherine herself from some moment in history when she had apparently been laughing.

She didn't need a key to crack the code of the other four. This young woman here, dark hair, wide-set eyes. That would be Patricia Langston in 20F, heading home after European travel. Lower spinal cord injuries. Never left the wheelchair to which AF801 had confined her and gone from this world entirely in just a few months.

Another young person. Catherine pulled the photo over to position it just to the right of Langston's. Adrian Janic, who sat so unknowingly in 18E. A carpenter from Serbia en route to an uncertain future, delivered to the most unexpected destination. Gone just after Langston, less than six months.

Nancy Whittle, 12B. Catherine looked at the round and heavy face, the bobbed hair. Mother of four from Kent, England. She'd cut herself off from family before taking her own life just after the first anniversary of the crash.

Douglas Marshall, 63B, Paris-based insurance executive, took a box cutter to his own throat.

Leaving Rostock. Dr. Rostock, who had survived the longest before laying waste to his world.

Catherine sat back at the table to breathe a little. Slowly in. Slowly out. Important to remember that she was in fact still breathing. These five had not been so lucky, but they suggested a pattern to her now. Left to right in the order of their deaths:

Langston, Janic, Whittle, Marshall, Rostock. Each one's injuries a degree less, each one also struggling all that much more with what lay beyond their bodies. Each had pushed a little closer to some elusive truth that Catherine had herself seen fluttering so often at the far reach of peripheral vision. She felt it in shivers, in the brush of black feathers, in the grainy video footage taken by a Warehouse camera far overhead.

She was home. There was only one thing now that could be done, she was certain. Was that Rostock gesturing from beyond the grave, touched by the finger of God: its placing, tracing and erasing? She would never have believed such things before, and did not quite believe them now. Not quite. But she couldn't deny or ignore the ghostly other source of inspiration. It lurked there at the edge of vision, moving now. Moving directly towards her.

She dressed in dark clothes. She found close-fitting leather gloves and a scarf to pull tightly around her throat. She pulled on a wool watchman's cap that she used when she ran in the winter. And she saw herself in the reflection of the living room window, cat burglar, girl spy. She gazed through her own features to the bright-lit shore beyond. A single yellow building there.

The city was pooled shadows and adorned with jewelled lights. The trees made patterns in the darkness, twigs and branches lacing overhead as she crossed the park. No cackling or cawing. No crows in sight.

She set out at 10:30 p.m., to honour the hour. A night breeze was sifting through the empty branches. She could hear them rustling, shivering and whispering against one another, a thousand voices. Smells too, her senses alive. Distant smoke, a fungal note. Algae on rocks. The background odour of fishy decay. Beach and trees. Botany. Biology. She crossed the park and emerged under the mercury gold of the street lights on the bridge.

She climbed the arc of the bridge, up under the flickering Deco lanterns. Turning seaward onto Beach Avenue, she had only a few blocks to walk to reach Nicola Street. And there she stood in front of the building she had admired for so many years. She was breathing very evenly. No nerves. Even her anger was stilled, as if the confrontation she was precipitating just then was more essential than anger could accommodate. She was at essentials now. Highly reduced, concentrated essentials relating to destruction, even death. And her body seemed to be reserving her adrenalin for future use.

She crossed the street, black Converse All Stars silent on the pavement. She walked in a steady line towards the glass front doors—the bank of buzzers, the nameplates. Inside a wall of mailboxes. The lobby was empty. Catherine peered in and considered options, then had the sensation of watching herself do something that she had not thought about and could not have predicted. As if controlled by someone else entirely, she pulled back from the glass, descended the steps. She went around the side of the building, into the alley. All the way back to the rear of the structure, where the recycling and the garbage bins sat solemn in the darkness. Beyond those, the hydro meter boxes. Taped behind one of them, a set of keys. Apartment 50.

Catherine was inside. She was in the elevator. And at the right door, the key slid into the lock and gave her the sense of returning, repeating an action that she had carried out so many times before.

The effect of being inside was intoxicating. She was surging with energies, buzzing yet oddly calm, the darkness inexplicably familiar. The apartment was much bigger and of course laid out differently than her own across the water. But she knew the rooms and surfaces. The long line of the bookshelves there. The sheen of the marble in the entrance foyer and the hardwood hallway stretching to the left towards the bedrooms at the back of the suite.

She felt the kitchen opening to her right. And she moved in that direction, running her hands along the counter edges, the smooth handles of the cabinets. On the counters, evidence of the busy person who ate on the fly as Catherine did herself. Starbucks instant coffee, Clif bars, packages of kimchi ramen. Catherine moved out through the kitchen's far door and into the dining room, then around the corner. And here she entered the living room, the apartment's main space.

It was much grander than any place she'd ever lived. And yet nothing about it seemed strange. Those bookshelves. Those sleek low chairs. The abstract paintings on the darkened walls, the Scandinavian glasswork, the square stone slabs around the fireplace. All things that she might herself have selected. And through the window that anchored the space, Catherine saw False Creek from the reversed view, looking south now instead of north. Here was a room of spectacular sunsets, Catherine thought, where the light would die operatically, glowing and then failing in these wood surfaces, winking in the glass and mirrors. *Red sky at night.*

To Catherine's left, through the living room, there was a small study with a writing desk, two computer monitors and a keyboard, more built-in shelves and a wide work surface covered in papers and photographs. Catherine fingered the papers and was again unsurprised to find evidence of the same focus that she herself typically brought to things. Evidence here of that same attention, that same gaze only directed back at her. Photos of the Warehouse. Many photos from inside: the teepee, the ping-pong table, the pods, the workstations. Photos of employees: Kalmar, Hapok, Arwen. Other things that really only she should know. DIY financial statements. Meeting agendas and minutes. A copy of a strategic plan that Catherine had not even shared with the leadership team. She wondered briefly who had seen that one. Morris, maybe? Had Phil? Wasn't Phil really the ultimate insider in the DIY story? He'd been there at the germinal moment with his subtle introduction of the ingestible battery. He'd guided her towards patents she needed to assemble. He'd even absented himself at crucial moments. Gone to Saturna Island so he didn't have to sign off on that original partnership agreement with Morris. Letting Stephanie Gorman take his place so that none of his other persuasions would have the look of conflict about them. He knew the upsides. He knew what DIY could be. He'd had the blueprint all along because she'd shared everything with him, and much of what she'd shared might as well have come out of Phil's own head.

Phil. Oh Phil. She was in a heightened sensory state. Streaming the moment in distinct smells and sounds and images. She was alive to every way in which she could take the measure of this space and situation. The way the light dissolved to shadow. The way the carpet smelled of fibre and must. The way the stainless steel refrigerator hummed in two distinct and assonant tones, a distant burble from the kitchen. Catherine thought of Phil again, wondering and wondering. Focusing with dark intensity. Could all this be Phil?

She was at the wide front window again. There was a faint gleaming, the suggestion of her own reflection, and the slopes of Kitsilano beyond. She hung in suspension over these images, cars whisking to the right and left along Beach Avenue below, the water seething black and silver. Across the way, the dim silhouette of buildings. Lights on in a random pattern. Orange. Grey. The blackest black. And behind the vertical blinds, next to her hand, a pair of binoculars on a tripod, presenting themselves for use at that perfect moment.

Catherine fixed on these with sudden understanding. They were at a certain height. They were aimed a certain direction. There could be no doubt about how they had been used and used again. She bent to them, slowly. Warm light. Sandy textures. A very long view. Without touching the instrument or the focus, she knew it immediately. Those lintels. Those blinds. She'd left them open and so all was plain. Ogden Avenue. Her apartment building. Her living room window. Her interior spaces. All there to see in the dusty low light.

Catherine's breathing slowed. Her body settled into what were now the obvious symmetries. Because there was a person in Catherine's apartment too. Of course, there had to be a person to complete the scene. Catherine watched through the binoculars and felt her focus sharpening, her limbs loose but ready. A person who moved into the room from the rear, coming down the short corridor that led to her bedroom. Walking calmly into space. First a darkness over bluish grey, then a clearer shape, reaching out, flicking on the apartment lights.

Ogden Avenue. Her space a glowing orange sphere. All details revealed. There she was, intensely more like Catherine Bach than Catherine's own reflection. The same curious face and resolute chin, the same way of folding the hands, the same height, weight. Red hair, check. Grey-green eyes, she was certain. Catherine watching and breathing, suffused in the moment, a sense of threat certainly, a sense of some ending to the story now onrushing. She should be afraid, she thought. But she was instead rising to the provocation. Kate Speir was in her apartment. Kate Speir with a kettle, boiling water, making tea. Kate Speir on the couch with her own Toby. Holding the phone. Using the phone. Catherine's complete replacement.

Less than a kilometre away across the cold darkness and the freezing waves, Catherine watched from a place that belonged to the other. Catherine gazing, observing. Infected by everything. And just that moment, Kate rose from the sofa and made her own way to Catherine's window. Her face now at the glass, eyes hooded with one hand. They were looking at one another. Their gazes met unmistakably. Met and held. Kate and Cate. Each one locked in apprehension of the other just as Catherine heard the sound of the front door opening far behind her. The figure in her own apartment shimmering, fading, vanishing. Now materializing as a voice in the hall in the apartment where she now stood. A woman's voice. A voice she knew. A man's voice too, muffled through the walls.

Doppelgänger, Ankou, Fylgia, Fetch.

I do not exist but for that which might wish to destroy me.

The voices had advanced into the kitchen of the apartment. The man and the woman. The light there came on, flooding into the dining room and partway towards Catherine in the still-darkened living room, with no thought of escape. She'd come that far across the distance, farther than the others. Catherine was the last one and she would complete this crossing. Her adrenalin in full release, her heart pounding, sweat on her arms, muscles tremoring with potential, hands balled into fists. Those shapes now sheathed around her, feathers, beaks and claws, the murmur of murder as the woman's silhouette appeared at the edge of the dining room, moving past the table and chairs, hand to the doorframe. Stopping there, everything shuddering from movement to utter stillness.

Catherine stepped forward. One stride and then another. Kate Speir did not retreat, did not speak or move. Her hands hung loosely at her sides. And even in the low light, Catherine could see the same woman she'd seen through the binoculars a moment before, those infinitely multiplying similarities between them. Fine features and a spray of freckles. Ginger hair. Emerald eyes. Deep reservoirs of resolve and a shared object of bottomless desire.

Catherine and Kate Speir, face to face in the silence, in the pixelated blue. Surely something ended here. And as if in response to that very thought—which seemed to emerge not from Catherine's consciousness at all, but to shape itself in the space between the two women—the vision again swept through her. The noise of the explosion and the roiling of black smoke in the cabin. The drink trolley smashing her legs. Pinned to the roof as her world tipped around her, poised at the top of that long fall. All that was solid in the world, all that was real, leached away. She saw the Warehouse dissolving upwards, pods and whiteboards ascending, artwork and ping-pong tables. Papers and estimates and best-laid plans, sifting upwards in fragments and particles, remnants and bits. The black hole once again did its work. Only this time it did not split her, it didn't deposit her on two sides of the universe at once. Catherine experienced instead a crushing unity in those seconds as she and Kate Speir held each other in their gaze. And around Catherine, those black shapes, thudding and beating their wings, those birds in their tightening shroud, their wings and beaks and claws touching her on the arms and legs and face, their shuddering bodies began to spiral inwards, re-entering her. And as they did so, they winked out of existence one by one, extinguishing themselves in the deep saline sea that was her own chest, her own heart.

Silence in the room. But now, a small movement. Kate Speir raised a single finger. *Wait here.* Then she turned and went back through the dining room and the kitchen.

Catherine was dizzy. Her ears ringing. She sank into a chair. And from the back of the apartment, somewhere near the doors, a short and muffled exchange.

I have to deal with something.

The man's response came in decisive tones. *Let me help.*

But Kate's voice was the firmer. *No. You have to leave, now.*

The sound of keys and a door closing. Soft footfalls. And then Speir was in the room again coming slowly towards Catherine, sitting opposite. A person sure of the decisions she'd made and proud of the results, her progress among the men who dominated her field. Her projects, including this one that brought the two of them together, the assembly of a great and complex thing that would change global security and surveillance practices more than any single program since the SR-71 spy plane. *Think of a spy plane that flies within.*

There had been nodding heads and impressed expressions around that boardroom table the day Speir announced it.

And now Speir found herself face to face in the reluctant light with the final piece of the puzzle she'd set out to complete. A woman so similar to herself that they might have been twinned. A woman whose expression suggested she'd been listening to Speir carefully for a very long time, perhaps so carefully as to have heard Speir's own thoughts.

Catherine Bach was the woman in question. And Kate Speir could see that she had arrived here furious, crazed with frustration. But that something new was minting itself in the room, something neither of them could have expected. They'd at last closed the distance between them. And when they were close enough to hear each other breathe, the symmetries of the moment were revealed by a mechanism that neither of them would ever fully understand, but to which they would thereafter, on occasion, silently acknowledge a debt of gratitude.

"I'm Catherine Bach," said Catherine.

"My name is Kate Speir," said Speir.

"I'm a survivor of Air France Flight 801," Catherine said.

Speir nodded. "I know," she said. "I've been told."

"What's really significant about that," Catherine said, "is the fact that there should have been no survivors."

Speir was looking at Catherine carefully. Finally, she said, "Well we can't always obey the laws of physics, now, can we?"

Catherine inhaled and exhaled. Big breaths. Perhaps it was, in the end, as simple as that: King needed Hawking as much as Hawking needed King. You had to break the rules that were unbreakable. To be human somehow depended on it.

Catherine on a bridge in the pouring rain. Catherine without a look back over her shoulder. In her apartment. Her couch, her teapot. Her cat Toby. Her black glass front window over which the blinds could now be slowly but firmly drawn.

FOUR

Near is
And difficult to grasp, the God.
But where danger threatens
that which saves from it also grows.

—FRIEDRICH HOLDERIN, "PATMOS"

BALLINACARRIG

SHE WALKED BACK TO HER OWN APARTMENT in the rain that broke when she left Kensington Place. Streets dancing and sparkling with the sudden deluge. Cars pluming through the shallow lakes that the overwhelmed storm sewers left along the curbs. She was soaked to the skin by the time she reached her own front door. Upstairs to an empty front room. A hungry tabby purring at her freezing ankles. She didn't check the bedroom or the closets. There was nobody there. It was just her and her own reflection in the black glass of her front window. Then she drew the blinds and that was gone too. She was alone.

She towelled off and fed Toby. Then she called Phil, because it was Phil to whom this announcement had to be made, one way or the other. "You should be the first to know," she said. "I'm sending Gorman the signed papers tomorrow. Mako wins."

That woke him up. What had happened?

"Phil, so much has happened," Catherine said. "I'm thinking I don't know the half of it. But for now, that's it. I'm done."

What else could she say? She felt guilt about the earlier flush of thoughts, the idea that this friend of fifteen years could have been working against her. But something had been amiss a long time. She might know even less in that moment than when it all began. And even if Phil had nothing to do with any of it, she wouldn't be able to help him understand that she'd been in that apartment, eye to eye with Kate Speir, realizing in a cyclonic second that she'd been desperately wrong about everything. That there was no other *her* in the room or in the world, no duplicate. And in their differences, Kate and Cate were safe, one from the other.

"Well," Phil said, "I'm surprised, I won't lie. But I'm glad you seem at peace with the outcome."

"Peace?" Catherine said. And while she tried to hide the bitterness she was feeling, it still came out as if she'd spat the word.

Phil pressed on, being Phil. So he was talking about her holidays now. The right thing for the moment. Get away. What about Maui? Seemed Phil had recently purchased a place there in Lahaina. Lovely beach, permanently good weather. She could get away and stay away as long as she pleased.

How convenient that she might vanish, Catherine thought.

"Take your sister," Phil was saying. "It can be a little dull on your own."

Catherine had to get off the phone. Enough decisions about places and people and objectives for one day. Sleep was taking her as she stood. So she hung up and she slept, deeply and without dreams. And in the morning, at breakfast with her sister, she didn't mention Phil or Maui at all, knowing the one would open into a hundred new questions and the other just didn't seem quite like the ending that the story of DIY required.

Valerie, for her part, sensed the sea change before Catherine said a word. Catherine could see her reading the new expression and body language. And when Catherine came clean and told Val that she'd sent a letter accepting the offer, her sister's own expression and body language were plain to read. Her shoulders slumped. Her mouth opened, then closed. Finally, she said, "I can't believe you're doing this. I can't believe you're letting go."

It was two years' worth of struggle that she was releasing, she wanted to say. To have come down from the clouds so sharply, to be set on such a delicate, unsustainable edge. No more black birds in Catherine's life. These were the things she wanted to but could not say to her sister.

Something different instead. Something she hoped had the ring of truth. "I dreamt up DIY, the idea, the concept. The dreaming is done. Now it's time for the rainmakers and the engineers."

Valerie was unconvinced. "I have to tell you I'm really disappointed."

"I'm sorry," Catherine said. "But do recall that you advised me to accept when Morris first made his offer."

"I know, I know. It's just"—Valerie was looking around for words—"anybody but Kate Speir."

"No, no," Catherine said, gently closing that line of conversation, turning to her slice of frittata and a cappuccino decorated artfully with ringlets and feathers of milk foam. Speir did not in the end deserve their animosity. Maybe she was building something that would make the world a far worse place. But she'd gone after DIY because that's what funds do. She'd stung the frog because that's what was in the scorpion's nature.

"So where do I go?" she asked her sister. "I mean, as in holidays?"

Valerie looked a little hurt. "It's the week before Christmas, babe. You know, you could take a break and spend it with family."

Catherine had entirely forgotten the season. And yes, it was upon them. Just three days to Christmas Eve. But Valerie never pushed. So she jumped in with alternatives. She was the perfect person to ask the holiday question. Vietnam. San Sebastian. "Maybe Puerto Rico," Valerie said. "San Juan is so beautiful."

Catherine went home and started packing for a trip without knowing where she was going. She packed for somewhere hot. Then she repacked for Europe. More like it. Museums and galleries. Go look at Venice before it sinks into the waves. And then, when almost everything she owned was packed into two enormous suitcases, she unpacked it all and fed Toby and sat watching CNN for several hours eating crackers and cheese. Yet another expert talking about AF801, as the second anniversary was on them. Still such curiosity, after all that time, all those months in which the mediasphere might have grown fixated on something else instead. Still the curiosity and innuendo, but this time with not one word said about survivors. Catherine was pleased about that, sitting there with a box of saltines and a package of jalapeno Jack slices.

At which point her own phone began to ring and ring and ring again. Hapok. Stunned that she would leave. He had looked up to her so much. He had admired her and worried that his style might have suggested otherwise. "Never had a boss like you, honest. I'm thinking of quitting."

Yohai all choked up. Engineer-kibbutznik Yohai manifesting real emotion. "I thought we shared a vision. I thought . . ."

There wasn't much to say. She just kept it simple. Mako Equity. New plans.

"Let's do something else," Yohai said. "Hire me again."

We'll see, she said. We'll see.

Kalmar too, eventually. It took him until late that afternoon. But then the phone vibrated warmly and there was beautiful Kalmar on the line. She didn't mind hearing that voice, and perhaps she even welcomed it more under these new circumstances. She was completely free, after all. No more CEO and the markets director to gossip about, to undermine morale.

"What'll you do, Red?" he asked her.

And it came to her suddenly that taking Kalmar to Maui might be just the thing to mark new beginnings. She wondered what Phil would think about that, then decided she didn't have to care and it wasn't his business anyway.

"Say, Kali," she said, leaning back on the sofa, her hand stroking Toby from between his ears, down his long back and to the end of his curling tail. And they talked about it at length. The area beaches. The potential to surf and dive. Though they never quite got to firm dates, as Kalmar had to deal with a couple things, sort out his schedule, he said he'd get back to her. And then neither of them had the time to linger as her phone was vibrating. Phil again. Catherine experienced a prick of conscience and irritation simultaneously, as if she'd been caught cheating by someone who had no claim to her at all.

"Yes?" she said, sounding quite annoyed. And she could hear it in the air between them immediately, before he even spoke. Phil was fussed and bothered.

Morris had been in touch. And Morris was inquiring about Kate Speir, who seemed to have vanished. Back to Seattle or Palo Alto or wherever she had originated. "It seems she's bailed," Phil said.

Catherine, who'd been lounging, was up sharply on her feet.

Mako Equity had written Morris and copied Phil's firm on their withdrawal from the acquisition of Parmer Ventures.

"That Mako-Parmer deal hadn't closed?" Catherine, more incredulous.

Apparently not. Morris had gloated far too soon. Speir had walked. So the whole thing reverted to what it had been before, which was something she'd want to think carefully about.

"You accepted his offer," Phil said. "He's legally bound."

"I do remember that," Catherine said.

"I'd advise that you not let him off the hook," Phil was saying. That might be hard for her to hear at just that moment. But Mako backing out would send strong negative market signals. DIY valuations would almost certainly fall, possibly by a lot. And that would make Morris's offer far richer than it had been by comparison. "Forget the *unicorn* for now," Phil was saying. "Just close this deal."

He was agitated. Breathing heavily on the line. But as she listened, Catherine was finding the signals crossed and confusing. If Phil really did have a stake in the Mako deal, it made sense that he might be in a panic. But she couldn't see why, under those circumstances, he'd call her to reveal the fact, to let her know his mood.

"Why are you telling me this, Phil?" she asked, before carefully considering those words.

There was silence on the line for a good stretch. Five seconds, maybe ten. And Phil's breathing had steadied by the time he spoke again. He'd processed something in those seconds that had given him a sudden, stable calm.

"Well," he said, "I would have thought that was obvious, Cate."

"Oh, listen . . ."

"No, no," he said, voice quieter now. "No, I do get it. Under your circumstances. The way all this went down."

"Phil, please . . ."

"I'm telling you this for the same reason I've ever told you anything," he said. "Because you're an old and valued friend."

"Of course," Catherine said. "I'm sorry if I . . ."

"But I'm also telling you now," Phil pressed on, "because I'm leaving."

"Leaving?" Catherine said. And now it was her breathing that was quickening, her pulse rising in her temples.

Leaving it all, he said. His practice. The city. The West Van prison. He didn't call it that, but that's how she heard it.

"Saturna Island," Catherine said. "You're moving there."

"Yes," he said. "It's been coming."

Probably years coming, he told her. He'd kept it to himself because people tended to talk you out of these things. Partners. Friends.

"We should meet for a drink. Do you have time?"

"Oh, gosh," Phil said. "I don't think so. Packing tonight. Christmas on the island. But it'll all be fine. Don't worry. We'll talk in the new year."

Then he got off the phone, the conversation cut short. Phil hung up and she stood there thinking about the advice he'd given. Take the inflated Parmer offer. Take the money that might not be there in six months. He didn't sound like a guy secretly on the far side of the deal. And ditching his life in the city after orchestrating such a thing didn't really seem like Phil's kind of common sense either.

She put her palms to her eyes and pressed. She took a deep breath, held it, exhaled. Then she phoned Stephanie Gorman, who thought Phil was maybe missing a key point.

"Great guy," Gorman said. "Love Phil. But valuations are voodoo."

The key point was that without Mako, Morris would struggle to complete the sale. "If he had the money himself he wouldn't have looked to Mako for support in the first place."

Maybe Phil was distracted, Gorman said. Maybe he had other things on his mind. But if Morris couldn't complete, then that left Catherine with two bad scenarios. "Sue someone who doesn't have the money to pay," Gorman said. "Or go back to a fifty-fifty with him and wait for Morris to go find another Speir in six months and do this all over again."

But there was a third way, of course. There always was. Option three: raise money and buy Morris out herself.

Gorman had a point, Catherine could see. And while she now had the strong urge to phone Phil back, to run Gorman's logic by him for vetting, that would be her phone buzzing again. And this time, it was Morris.

"Stephanie, you may well be right," she said. "But hang with me for a few hours here. I will call you later."

What Morris had in mind, he said when Catherine picked up, had less to do with one of them buying the other out at all. He was thinking more along the lines of tearing up and rewriting the partnership agreement entirely. Same share split as before, better separation provisions for her.

"That buy-sell is not the best deal for the smaller partner," he explained.

"Oh, you think?" Catherine said.

"Listen, listen," he said, and she could hear the squelch of him shifting in his leather swivel office chair. "We've been together three years. There have been disagreements, but a lot of real progress has also been made. DIY is sitting on an incredible product. We're nearly ready to beta. Kudos to you."

Catherine was preparing. She was applying flame to an answer so that it would be both burnt black and searing hot when she handed it to him. But Morris plowed on ahead of her, filling phone space, and she waited to see how deep a hole this man would dig for himself. Morris was asking her now to pretend the offer had never happened. Speir was gone. And yes, that put Morris in the tricky position of not having financial backing for his offer. But don't punish him for the takeover attempt. It hadn't been his idea. Speir hadn't even been his contact, Morris said. He'd never himself actually met the woman or anyone from Mako.

"Sorry, what?" Catherine said. "You never met her?"

Morris was stammering and backpedalling, sidestepping, tripping over himself. It wasn't his place to say exactly how it had all gone down. But yes, there was somebody else involved, okay? A third party had brought Mako to the table. A third party had done all the negotiating and the face-to-face.

"Run that by me again," Catherine said. "A third party?"

None of his doing, Morris was saying. Yes, the offer finally took the form of a Parmer buyout. But that was all brokered by somebody else.

"Who, Morris?" Catherine said. "Tell me."

"Someone helped her." Morris, increasingly frantic. "But I can't say more. I'm completely outside of this thing. Nobody is returning my calls. Not Mako. Nobody at DIY. But you have to understand, Catherine, all cards on the table: I don't have the funds to complete my offer, and I wouldn't for many months."

Catherine had been pacing as they spoke. But as these last words sank into her, she was at her window. She was staring across those grey waves to the far shore, to the building, the blinds wide open in that suite on the top west corner. Nobody standing where she had stood that night. Nobody standing where she'd heard those voices. Kate Speir and the man who had wanted to provide such crucial assistance. A voice Catherine knew. The exact words too. *Let me help.*

Her fingers were on the windowpane. It was cold outside and the gulls were screaming. She stood frozen for several seconds. And then the sudden inner thaw. Rapid and relieving.

Speir herself had said it. Speir had directed them both to the finding. The significant factual statement that could be made about AF801 was that there was a survivor. Catherine Bach. And she was supposed to be alive.

"Catherine, listen," Morris began.

"Morris," Catherine said, finally. "Your offer has been accepted and payment is due. If you want to discuss different arrangements, come to Vancouver. Tomorrow late morning works for me."

Then she phoned Stephanie Gorman back with her last big idea, which she thought was also the worst idea of all for being so risky, but to which Gorman agreed in exactly one second.

Going back to those same bankers with the reassuring addition of a man in the deal was hard on Catherine's pride. But those three in their dark suits agreed to meet. And that very afternoon, they further agreed to a six-month bridge loan if Gorman's husband and the Kaizen Forum co-signed the note.

"This is a great deal for everyone except my client, right?" Stephanie Gorman said to the bankers. "You're lending us bridge money against security from a third party. Like her company, her effort, her sweat equity is worth what, exactly?"

In that high boardroom, outlook on urban Vancouver and the impossible mountains beyond.

"Stress on the word *bridge*," the sandy-haired one said, shooting cuffs with those T-bone cufflinks. "After six months, your client has to be on the far side. We're paid out or I'm afraid you're out of the frying pan and into the fire."

They all laughed at that. Catherine didn't laugh. And Gorman didn't laugh either. Then they pushed a loan agreement across the table towards both of the women. They talked among themselves about boats and road biking. And when it came time for Catherine and Stephanie Gorman to leave, the bankers shook Gorman's hand firmly but Catherine's with much more caution, as if she were a delicate and possibly poisonous flower.

"Regards to your husband," said the one to Gorman. "Merry Christmas."

And the women were then in an elevator and dropping fast after what seemed like about ten minutes since they'd arrived.

"Morons," Gorman said, after a few seconds of silence. "You'll be worth more than all of us combined one day."

Catherine looked over at the older woman. She had her eyes up on the screen in the top corner of the car just as Phil had that day in Chicago. All that news, all the time. Markets and global affairs, things dropping to earth and things aflame.

"Thank you," Catherine said.

"You're welcome," Gorman said. "Six months of financing and we need to get you to market. Now go close with Morris."

He called the next morning. Morris in a foreign airport two days before Christmas Eve. He was climbing into a car, coming into town. She could have flown to him, of course. But she'd been to Chicago twice in a month. Morris could bloody well fly to her.

"Go get him," Valerie said when Catherine called to tell her.

"I will," Catherine replied. "I'm going to be that woman with the snakes for hair."

She met him in a Starbucks just to lower any expectations he might have. In Vancouver, the weather had warmed and the place was flooded with sun. But Morris had worn heavy clothes, suitable for the Chicago Christmas cold. They were squeezed into a corner next to the cream and sugar station. Christmas jazz was playing on the stereo, the air cloying with the scent of gingerbread and eggnog lattes. The place was jammed with Christmas shoppers and Morris was sweating. If she was indeed Medusa, Morris seemed to know it instinctively and kept his eyes off her face, over her shoulder and out towards the front door. She kept up an uncomfortable line of questioning about Kate Speir, and about Morris's implied complicity in releasing confidential information to an outside financial interest. About camaraderie, trust, business ethics and of course signed and witnessed nondisclosure agreements.

Morris squirmed and sweated and struggled to answer. Then he finally cracked and said it again: "Kate, I just don't have the liquidity. You press on with this if you like, but you can't get blood from a stone."

She sighed elaborately and actually looked at her nails. Morris was melting in the warm afternoon sun, barely touching the chai he'd ordered. She waited, then waited a bit more. Then she tabled her offer to pay Morris out of the picture, for good.

Morris rocked back in his chair, his expression fixed in a grimace of surprise as it might have been during acute myocardial infarction. But Catherine knew Morris was not going to die there in that café. You didn't die from the shock of having your bacon undeservedly saved. And while the money might have been half what Morris had originally offered her, he was going to recover from his rictus here and take that money over getting sued. For a moment Catherine wished those bankers could have witnessed the moment. But on only a nanosecond's review, she knew it would never feel better than this, to have closed the matter on her own.

And on paper, in any case, the *sitch* was exactly that clear. The matter was now closed. And when she had slid that term sheet across the table to Morris in that crowded, overheated Starbucks, "Jingle Bell Rock" playing several notches too loud, she knew that DIY was hers alone.

For better or worse. For richer or poorer. A contest won not by fighting, but by walking away.

Or almost. There remained one matter. Because she did still need answers, and it was now clear to her that only one person had them. So late lunch was arranged for that same day. And despite the fact that he'd made plans for Christmas and was leaving the city that evening, he agreed to meet when she insisted.

"I thought we'd talked about going to Maui," Catherine said.

Kalmar shrugged and gestured. "It came up unexpectedly. These plans."

"For what, Kalmar?"

"Whistler," he said. "With friends."

The man whose face she had long admired, coming in through the crowds in that hipster brewery in Japantown: brown glass growlers and charcuterie plate with pâtés and salamis. He looked the same as always: her urban mystic. But Catherine could feel the tremor of his leg bouncing under the table. She saw the anchor tattoo as his hand went up to his face unconsciously to conceal now-nervous lips. And in the end, despite feeling Medusa surge again within, Catherine realized she didn't want Kalmar dead. Part of her was still too disappointed. So she ate rabbit pâté and pickles and listened to the room around them. He didn't touch his food. He seemed to be waiting for her to speak.

"I talked to Kate Speir," she said, finally.

He didn't do a Morris. No startled response. He didn't lean back or widen those ice-blue eyes. If anything, he seemed to settle there across plates and glass and flatware. He put both his hands on the table, loose fists. He didn't look at her directly, but gazed attractively towards the front window, his eyes glinting with the sunny action there. He was entertaining responses, Catherine thought. Calculating how much she knew, as something more serious flitted there under the surface, the shadow of a trout in cold river water.

"So?" Kalmar started. "How did you get along?"

"Don't do it, Kali," Catherine said. And she felt a genuine sadness just then. "Please. Just don't."

He looked at her. Those blue eyes bruised around the lids now too. Tired blue. "What then, Catherine?" he said. "Maybe you go first."

"You're not eating," she observed.

He picked up a gherkin and held it to his teeth.

"Kimchi ramen," she said.

He didn't bite. He put the gherkin down. He looked away again, this time with a wistful smile. Instant noodles and Clif bars brought to the women in his plans. He had a sure fondness for helping, for fetching, for ingratiating himself. *Let me help.* An Icelandic mystic in search of his package. What were the chances that all that familiar food in Speir's kitchen had come direct from the DIY canteen? Why wouldn't it have? Kalmar was a man who'd stolen more important things than that. Catherine had made it possible by being more open with him than anyone else. Perhaps Kate had too. Perhaps they'd both exposed themselves. And how skilfully Kalmar had worked the angles as they were presented to him, instructing both of them on the topic of invasive species. Kate and Cate. Both of them listening in their different ways, from their perfectly reciprocal positions on either side.

Catherine thought she could picture the scene exactly. Yaletown over fancy plates. Pork with miso and Hiroshimana greens. Clicking chopsticks and conversation all around. Light fixtures like planets, like a galaxy in which the diners were suspended. The sake would be poured. And Kalmar would have been there in his suit, with his lean frame, his brooding slouch, attentive eyes. Catherine herself had so nearly gone under. Speir, for her part, would have looked at Kalmar and licked her lips. He was so eager to help. So keen to please. But there was apparently a line even Kate Speir wouldn't cross. And she'd reached it in her own living room, facing, finally, the survivor who was meant to survive.

Kalmar sipped his water, then put it down. "Just business," he said. "I'm sorry."

"Don't be," Catherine said. "But where did your business go?"

Kalmar again looked away, the lowering light making shadows across his features.

"The leak," she said. "That was Mako bait, was it?"

No answer.

"Did you do other bad things, Kalmar? Did you show them confidential meeting minutes and financial statements? Did you break the law?"

His jaw tightened and his hands tensed again on the table.

"You got to know her. Why do think she'd pull out?" Catherine asked.

Kalmar freezing, his expression hardening further. Then he swivelled his gaze to look at Catherine squarely. He still had the juice, Catherine thought. She could feel the movement of something in her own chest. She could feel the full impact of being engaged by this man.

"She pulled out because of you," Kalmar said, eyes still intensely locked on her own. Was that real emotion brimming there?

Catherine waited.

"She told me about meeting you," Kalmar said. "Wouldn't say where or what about."

Catherine listening only.

"What did you talk about?" Kalmar was now asking. "What the hell did you say?"

Catherine in silence, now seeing quite clearly how it must have happened after their Kensington Place exchange. Kate Speir telling Kalmar the news. She was pulling out. He'd reached a hand to touch her. *Listen, listen.* And Speir had slapped him hard. Right there on that left cheek. Catherine could see it as if in a vision. Speir was small, but very strong. Fair skin, red hair, a green-eyed fighter. And Kalmar had shrunk back from her.

Kalmar with something like fear in his eyes now. Kalmar afraid of his own future and turning away to conceal the shame of it. Kalmar turning away.

There was nothing more that needed to be said. He'd get the letter. He'd accept the settlement. He wanted now just to be gone. And he left without even another glance in her direction. Kalmar up and heading for the door, slipping and slouching towards the street. She'd never see him again. She was sure of that. She'd never see Kate Speir either, but then Speir, by her nature, did not wish to be seen.

So it wouldn't be Maui where Catherine decided to go for her much-needed break forty-eight hours later. Not Vietnam. Not Puerto Rico or Spain. They had a big party at the Warehouse the next day. Hapok hired a mariachi band, because he said no more goddamn Christmas covers and because today they stood with Mexico. They had a mountain of tacos and many bottles of Dos Equis Amber. There were high-fives. And there were hugs. There was hardly any talk of the beta release, which would need to be accomplished soon. Time now for beer and food and a long, deep breath. One carol, Hapok conceded, ordered up and sung with Yohai using the new house karaoke system, a nod to where Catherine was going: "Christmas in Killarney."

Directly home and to bed. Directly to the airport in the morning with a single carry-on bag and a lumpy envelope in her purse, travelling with the crowds on Christmas Eve. There was "Last Christmas" trickling down from a thousand invisible speakers, silver wreaths on the pillars and an arrangement of penguins on a fake iceberg just outside of international departures. Everyone at YVR security offered a greeting. *Merry Christmas, Happy Holidays, Happy Hanukkah, Eid Milad Saeid.*

A seat in the lounge, a ticket to Dublin, and one last call to make.

"May I speak to Phil?" she said, when a stranger answered at his number.

"Oh, he's shovelling," the woman said, and laughed. "On Christmas Eve!"

"Oh," Catherine said. "All right. I'm Catherine."

"Catherine," the woman said. "I know you, yes."

"Have we met?"

"No, no. This is my first time in Canada. I'm Camila, a friend of Phil's. Let me get him."

No don't, Catherine said. I mean, not right this second. Christmas Eve and all. Let him do the shovelling. Did they really have snow?

Camila laughed again. Not snow. Manure. For the plants in the greenhouse. Did she know about Phil's plants? Well yes, he was out there now shovelling manure with Daniel.

"Daniel is my son," Camila said. "He has come with me." Visiting from Spain, Camila said. Her father had known Phil's father from long ago. Let me get him, Camila said again. They were just down at the bottom of the orchard. No trouble to get him.

"No, no," Catherine said. "Tell Phil I'm boarding a flight."

Okay. Okay. She would tell Phil that.

"Tell him Merry Christmas," Catherine said. "And to you too, Camila."

"Yes," Camila said. "Merry Christmas, Catherine. Merry Christmas and the happiest new year."

Catherine in a departure lounge. And then in motion. Dublin direct. But no big rush. Christmas Day in the city. White lights in

strands over Grafton Street. Fireworks on a barge in the Grand
Canal. She had a pint with some Australians in Kehoe's and a long
walk by herself down City Quay, thick snowflakes falling and melting on the cobbles. She woke in the green light of Boxing Day.
Rented a car. Headed west, then south. A night in Abbeyleix. A
long, slow drive east through Carlow to the coast. To Arklow and
north. Everything was closed but she found the lockbox for the
Airbnb she'd rented from Vancouver. A cottage near the beach in
Ballinacarrig, where she woke on the second anniversary of something important that had once happened quite near to there. Brittas
Bay. Air France Flight 801. She could walk to the sand, to the very
spot where she had come ashore. And after coffee, she did that.
There on the beach, that morning, she walked and found her place,
then stood and stared up at the sky. She stared up at the perch from
which she had fallen. Soft sea swells from the Irish Sea. Very high
cirrus clouds, the most delicate white lace against a dusty blue. The
beach grass on the rolling dunes sifted in a cold wind. The sun was
blazing but it did not do much to warm her. And looking up she
saw that it was also circled in a wide halo that winked and refracted
light, suggesting that the sun was itself not the largest orb in the
sky, but the burning white centre of a shimmering, larger sphere.

Ice crystals in the ionosphere, Catherine knew, suggesting rain to
come. But for the moment, not merely meteorology, auspicious also.

Catherine was on one knee, her small offering in hand. Here the
pebbles were strewn across the sand in a way that suggested constel-
lations. She kneeled in a galaxy of stones, the beach seeming to mirror
in its patterns the heavens above. She kneeled at this point of meeting,
where she herself had met the earth after her own terrifying fall.

She had brought things. Crucial things that could be carried no
farther. A broken watch. A flight safety card. An envelope of photographs. She had sealed these in a Ziploc bag that she laid in a hole
she'd dug with her hands in the sand. She released these back into

the wilds from which they had been plucked and assigned such significance. Now they could return to insignificance, or be adopted into new matrices of meaning by someone else if they were discovered. Let them charge a new imagination. They were gone from hers.

One final item.

Tear-stained. Wrinkled. She unfolded it now as she had so many times before, its creases darkened with the oils of her hands, the image smudged, but the yellow highlighter plain. That seat plan. Those lucky seats. The sacred six.

But she did not read the coordinates again, or recite the seat numbers aloud. That liturgy had been said a final time, addressed to the gods who had authored her presence there, the sole survivor. Gods who were so near and yet ungraspable. She folded the paper up again, lengthwise, to fashion a taper. And then she set it on fire with matches she'd picked up at a gas station in Bray, watching the flare of flame, the tendril of smoke in the salty air.

The flame burned down. She felt the heat rising. And just as it threatened to scorch her fingertips, she dropped it, watching the ashes and embers scatter in the Irish sand.

ACKNOWLEDGEMENTS

Thanks Martha Kanya Forstner and everyone at Doubleday Canada and Penguin Random House Canada. Thank you Dean Cooke and everyone at the Cooke Agency. I consider it a great fortune to work with such warm and intelligent friends.

Catherine Bach quotes on several occasions from the book *ReWork*, written by Jason Fried and David Heinemeier of 37SIGNALS. Thanks to them for an inspiring work and its influence on that character.

I would like to acknowledge the invaluable gifts of love, friendship and wisdom that I received from those people I lost in 2016, the year this book came together. I will never forget you, but will remain grateful and in your debt.

Finally, thanks to my family, who have stood by me and supported me through difficult times. *Where danger threatens, that which saves from it also grows.*